a life, redefined

also by Tracy Hewitt Meyer

The Reformation of Marli Meade

a life, redefined

a Rowan Slone novel

TRACY HEWITT MEYER

bhc
press™

Livonia, Michigan

Editor: Joni Firestone
Proofreader: Hannah Ryder

A LIFE, REDEFINED

Published by BHC Press

Library of Congress Control Number: 2017941236

ISBN: 978-1-64397-012-7 (Hardcover)
ISBN: 978-1-64397-013-4 (Softcover)
ISBN: 978-1-64397-014-1 (Ebook)

For information, write:
BHC Press
885 Penniman #5505
Plymouth, MI 48170

Visit the publisher:
www.bhcpress.com

for my mom

When the darkness is too great,
When the pain is too real,
There is nothing but sharp edges,
Razor slices,
To remind me that I am alive.

~ Rowan Slone ~

a life, redefined

chapter one

"ROWAN SLONE." Mr. Chambers, my biology teacher, stood at the front of the classroom, peering at me over wire-rimmed bifocals. "You are paired with Mike Anderson. And please try to sit up straight." With cheeks aflame, I pushed my butt back in the seat and straightened my spine.

"Does anyone have any questions?" he asked.

No one answered, already shoving books into backpacks. At the first clang of the bell, students bolted out of seats and out of the room, their brain space already occupied with the next class. But I stayed behind. I hadn't meant to nearly fall asleep in class. I just wasn't sleeping well these days or these past several years. Feeling like my skinny arms weighed two hundred pounds, I pushed my own books into my bag. I would apologize to Mr. Chambers. With one year until graduation, now was not the time to get on a teacher's bad side.

Then I heard my name.

"Hey, Rowan. I guess we're partners, eh?"

Standing in front of me was Mike Anderson, my new biology partner, high school senior, and member of the varsity soccer team. *And* the one guy whose image always popped into my head when I thought about the perfect male specimen.

"Um, yeah." I cleared my throat and picked up the book I'd just dropped on my foot. "I guess we are."

"When should we start? The report is due at the end of the month, and I'm a terrible writer."

Mike's pine-colored eyes peered down at me as I fumbled for an answer. Something about him took my thoughts, jumbled them into a solid mass, and threw them out of my head. I really did need more sleep.

"Rowan? Are you okay?"

My chuckle rang shriller than I liked. "I can start anytime. I work after school, but…um…I have a library pass and we can work on it here at school until nine. On weeknights."

His dark brows rose. "A library pass? What's that?"

My lips pulled upward. Was that a smile on my face? Whatever it was, the uncomfortable feelings from a moment ago withered, if not away, then further back in my mind. Talking to him wasn't *so* difficult.

"A library pass. You can apply for one in the office. It's for students who want to study in the evenings." And stay out of their houses for as long as possible.

"Huh. Sounds cool." His tone didn't support the statement.

I shoved another book in my bag, wishing this conversation was over. Or that it would go on forever. Or that I could come across a little bit more interesting than being a library nerd.

"So, how about tomorrow?"

I didn't bother to check my calendar. "Sure. I can meet tomorrow. Can you be here around seven? I work until six."

"Yep. I'll meet you out front." He laughed. "I don't think they'd allow me into the school after hours if I tried to get in by myself since I've never actually been *in* the library."

Still laughing, he strode toward the door, bag slung over one shoulder, his jeans falling *just right* over his hips.

I let out a whoosh of breath and followed him.

I STUMBLED through the masses of kids and headed toward my locker, feeling a very distinct yet unfamiliar thumping in my chest. Mike Anderson and I had been in school together for years, though he was a senior and I was a junior. Actually, we should've both been seniors, but I had to repeat the fifth grade-the same year my baby brother, Aidan, died—the same year my world turned upside down.

I made it to my locker just as my best friend, Jess, came clomping toward me. I don't know if she meant to stomp or if it was her heavy, military-styled boots that gave extra weight to each of her slender legs.

"Hey, Ro." She pushed the tortoise-shell glasses up her nose. "Guess what?"

"What?" I turned the combination on my locker.

"Dad's out of town this weekend. And guess who's coming over?" Her voice went all sing-songy and I rolled my eyes.

"Let me guess." I yanked out my next book and slammed the door. "Paul."

She grabbed my arm and bent down to look me in the face. Jess was several inches taller than me, as most people were. I was only five-foot-two, not to mention I was trapped inside the body of a prepubescent boy. Or at least I thought so. Jess was at least five-foot-six. And the heels on her boots gave her another two that she really didn't need.

"I can't wait. Ro, you have to meet him!"

"I have met him. He was my substitute teacher last year in art class."

She narrowed her blue eyes, heavily rimmed in black liner. "Don't start." She waved her hand in the air and her face morphed back into an expression of bliss. "Ro, you really have to get to know him. He's just so, well, *cool!* And he's really not that much older than us!" Her blood-red lips pulled wide over her white teeth.

I sighed. "What do you see in someone that old?" We started toward English class.

"First of all, he's not that much older than us. He's only twenty-five. And second of all, he's not teaching anymore, so there's no problem."

"Other than he's twenty-five and you're seventeen!"

She snorted and bumped me with her hip, sending me sprawling to the side. She caught me by my arm and continued, "Promise you'll meet him again? Give him a chance?"

Jess had been my best friend since the ninth grade when we had physical education together. During a field day event, we were paired in the two-legged race. Being so much taller than me, especially with the added height of her very un-field-day style boots, she ended up practically carrying me across the finish line because my short legs couldn't keep up. We'd been friends ever since.

"I'll give him a chance." I went to my seat.

"HAVE YOU thought about my offer?" Dan, my boss, slid along the counter toward me. He glanced around the small, empty office and leaned over my shoulder. "Are you going to go out with me or not?" His laugh grated on my nerves even though I think he meant it to be soft.

I moved down the red laminate counter, the edge cutting into my stomach, and started gathering papers: work orders, invoices, bills of sale; all the paperwork that came with a used car business. Dan was the owner, and I was the after-school employee. He was thirty. I was seventeen.

Dan drummed his fingernails, short and clean, on the top of an auto magazine with the picture of a Mustang emblazoned across the front. His eyes were on me as I stapled receipts to invoices and piled them in the metal basket.

"You haven't sold many cars this month," I said.

"I know." He waved his hand dismissively. "It's okay. I'll make up for it this summer." He leaned over. "Come on, Rowan. Let's go out. It'll be fun. You're almost eighteen, right? Close enough." The smell of his breath, a mixture of peppermint gum and the cigarette he allowed himself in the afternoon, wafted through the air.

This time I slid to the other side of the counter. "Don't be a nag, Dan. You don't talk to Mrs. Ames like this do you?" Mrs. Ames was the elderly woman who helped him during the day; my ancient counter-part, you could say.

He laughed again and picked up the magazine. "You'll come to your senses soon enough." He walked outside to greet a customer.

It was almost six o'clock. In just a few minutes the car lot would close and I could leave. I had to pick up my sister, Trina, from cheerleading practice, but then I could go home and brain-storm ideas for the biology report…and think about what I wanted to wear when I met Mike at the library tomorrow.

My thoughts were interrupted when Jess burst through the door, Dan following close behind.

"Hey, Ro." She sauntered to the counter and leaned on her elbows. She glanced at Dan wearily then promptly ignored him.

"Hey, Jess. Done with work?"

"Yeah. Mr. Sumners told me I could leave. Something about needing me early tomorrow to sort new inventory."

Jess worked at the used bookstore on Main Street.

"Can I have a ride home when you're done? Dad has to work late. Again." She popped her pink chewing gum and pulled a strand of cherry-red hair through her fingers.

"Yep. Dan, do you need me for anything else?"

"Nope." He retreated to his personal office. "You're good. Go on." He shut the door.

"Come on." I grabbed her wrist and pulled her out the door and into a warm, spring evening.

It was April in Appalachia, and the world was blushing green. Flower buds spurted out of brown limbs and soon the area would be awash in bright colors–yellow, white, red, blue. I had always loved spring for its simple hopefulness. There was nothing that could brighten the lives of people in this old town, but I loved that nature tried every single year without fail.

"He creeps me out." Jess glanced behind us where the car lot office sat—a small, perfectly square building that rose out of the ground like an enormous porta-potty.

"Nah. He's not so bad. I guess." I didn't tell her that the closer I got to eighteen, the more he amped up his flirting.

"Yeah, right. He creeps me out."

"Do you want me to take you home or somewhere else?" I unlocked my car, a tiny, used number my dad had bought from Dan last year.

"Home, please. I have to call Paul. He just started a new job."

Jess kept talking, but her voice morphed into a dull drone while I thought about the biology report. It was due in four weeks. Tomorrow we'd have to pick a topic. And then we'd have to meet several times to get the report done.

This could mean meeting at least two to three times a week, especially if he wasn't comfortable with writing. That would equal a lot of time before the paper was due. A lot of time together. Sitting side-by-side. Talking. Getting to know each other.

"Earth to Rowan…" Jess was staring at me.

"Huh?" I shook my head. "Were you saying something?" I eased onto the road.

"Uh, yeah. What were you thinking? You were a million miles away." She leaned forward until her face filled my peripheral vision. "You're not thinking about a guy, are you?"

I turned my face toward the side window. "No. Don't be silly."

"Is everything okay at home?"

I sighed heavily. "No. I mean, yes. Everything's fine. I guess I'm just tired." I yanked my sleeves over my hands and clutched the steering wheel to keep from rubbing my left arm, the place where I'd carved a dozen angry lines over the years. Just because I didn't take a razor to my skin anymore didn't mean the urge didn't pop up every now and then.

Jess rambled on about Paul the entire way to her house, and I couldn't remember a single thing she'd said as she hopped out of the car. I drove home feeling like I'd had a gallon of coffee, though I hadn't had any caffeine all day. My mind was alert, but almost manic, unable to focus on any one thing. Instead I kept flipping between thoughts of biology class, Mike, Dan and his flirting, back to Mike, to biology…back to Mike.

I turned onto our dirt driveway and pulled to the side of our small, ranch-style house. My dog, Levi, came bounding toward me with tongue hanging out until his long leash stopped him.

"Hey, boy." I dropped to my knees.

Levi was a large dog, about eighty pounds, with brown fur and big, brown eyes. He showed up on our property three years ago and Dad had said we could keep him. It was one of the most surprising things Dad had ever done for us. Perhaps the only *nice* thing he'd ever done.

"Did you have a good day, pal?" Levi flopped onto his back. "Did you find some squirrels to harass? Maybe some birds? Hmmm?" His dark doggie lips pulled into a smile.

"I'll be back in a minute, boy." I gave him one last pat and moved toward the house, my footsteps becoming heavier and more resistant with each step. Our home looked like many other middle-class families' homes in this rural area. It was brick, built around the 1960s. But it had its differences. The curtains were always pulled tight. The gutter was loose on one side. And the grass, what patches there were of it, was perpetually brown.

"Mom? I'm home." I eased through the front door, careful not to let it slam. I spoke quietly in case she was in bed, which she most likely was. There were no lights on so I flipped a few switches. Silence was heavy and my stomach rumbled. I zipped up my hoodie as I moved toward the hall.

I paused by my bedroom and threw my bag on the bed. Mom hadn't willingly left the house in seven years, ever since my brother died. Every now and then she ventured out to see a doctor about her failing health, which now included diabetes and obesity. Or once a year she attended some school function for me or my sister. But mostly she stayed home in bed.

"Mom?" I turned the knob to her bedroom door and pushed it open. She was lying on top of the bed, right in the middle where her ample body had made a permanent indentation. How Dad, who was a tall man, found the room to sleep beside her, I'd never know. An old quilt Gran had woven was thrown over her feet. She was snoring, her brown hair disheveled and sweaty. The television was muted. I eased the door closed and went into the kitchen to make a sandwich.

With stale bread in hand, I walked back outside. "Levi!" He nuzzled my hand as I sat down on the grass. "You want a bite, boy?" He licked my fingers. "Okay, but just this once."

A truck pulled in. My dad was home.

I hunched over Levi, pulling my knees into my body, trying to blend in with him. I was far enough around the side of the house that Dad might not see me.

He got out of his black pick-up truck and walked forward on solid, heavy feet. With short, dark hair and hazel eyes, I could see where a different man used to dwell there. During one of Mom's more nostalgic moments, she'd laugh about how she fell in love with Elvis Presley. Now, though, Dad's face, after years in the Army, and the past ten as a prison guard, had become wrinkled, sallow; his hair liberally streaked with gray.

He stopped mid-stride. "Is dinner ready?" His head turned like it was on a pivot, his body held rigidly toward the house.

I shrugged and rubbed my arm. "No. Mom is asleep." I held my breath. "Want me to make you something?" I asked quickly.

He stared at me, his eyes hard. Not bothering to answer, he walked through the door. "Amy! Get out of that bed!"

The screen door slammed shut behind him, but the thud of Dad's booted steps reverberated across the yard.

"Amy!"

I cringed at the sound of Dad's heavy fists beating against the bedroom door. I pulled out my cell phone, a hand-me-down from my dad when I started driving and took over all the household errands.

I looked at the yard with its bare patches and long-stretches of shadow; at the world around me with its steep mountains, constructing a landscape that was beautiful, intimidating and mysterious. The sun was setting behind the largest mountain, casting pastel streaks across the sky. A hawk soared high overhead, its colors indistinguishable in the fading light.

The house quieted and the only thing I heard through the screen door was the sound of dinner being prepared–cupboards opening and closing, silverware and plates being set. Then a car pulled in. Someone was dropping off my sister. I'd forgotten to pick her up.

My heart stopped. *Please don't let Dad see that someone else had to bring her home.* He didn't come out of the door, though.

But that thought was quickly forgotten when I saw who was behind the wheel. Mike Anderson. Why was *he* bringing her home?

Trina threw open the car door and jumped out. She flashed me a smile that was a little too big, a little too pleased. "Bye, Mike! Thanks for the *ride!*"

She slammed the door and did a little skip in her cheerleader's uniform, the skirt barely covering her butt and the top so short her stomach was exposed. "Hi, Rowan." Her voice was full of sugar. "Have a nice day at work?"

Levi growled as she bounced up the stairs, her long blond hair swishing against her back. Mike's car stayed in our driveway long after the door slammed behind my sister, but I couldn't look up.

Why was *he* giving Trina a ride? Was it only because I had forgotten to get her? Would that put the smirk on her face?

There was nothing between Mike and me. There never had been. We'd known each other for years and you could say we were friends, casual friends. Acquaintances. But for me, seeing Trina get out of his car caused bile to rise in my throat.

Gritting my teeth, I flipped opened the phone and searched my contacts until I found Dan's cell number.

I took my time typing out the text:

> Maybe we should go out. I'll be 18 in 3 weeks.
> We can go out then.

Happy birthday to me.

chapter two

MY ALARM went off at five forty the next morning. If I didn't get into the shower before Trina, who took an hour and a half to wash, primp and do what God only knows, I'd have to wait until night. And today I had other plans after work. Namely, a library date with Mike.

But thinking of that meeting didn't bring the same wobbly knees it did yesterday. Now each time I thought about him, his image was replaced with Trina's smug face as she tumbled out of his car. Not very pleasant. No, not very pleasant at all.

Still, I went into the bathroom, shut the door without a sound and turned on the water. Soon the mirror clouded and fog swirled toward the overhead light. I stepped into the shower and let the scalding water burn red streaks onto my skin.

I washed my hair, face, then my body, keeping the strokes light over the scars on my left arm, a habit I'd developed when I used to cut myself. But I hadn't done that in a few years. Three, to be exact.

The first time I did it, I had just turned eleven. My baby brother had been dead a month and Mom and Dad had gotten into another ear-splitting fight. Who knew what it was over that time? The only solace I had found, as I huddled on the bathroom floor, was the old razor from Dad's toiletry kit.

But I didn't cut anymore.

I turned off the water and got out of the shower. Wiping a circular clearing in the foggy mirror, I studied my reflection. Water streamed out of my long, light brown hair and over my thin shoulders. My eyes were an indeterminate mix of blue and gray; like a stormy sea, my Gran always said.

My skin was pale and my cheekbones prominent. I had a small frame, petite as Gran called it, with my collarbones protruding sharply and my ribs easily identified. But there *was* beauty there, if I was honest with myself. Would Mike see it? Or would he just see a mousy little girl who was a better writer than him and the road to a higher grade?

Did he really like my sister or was she just taunting me? But then, why did *he* bring her home?

Trina pounded on the door, not loud enough to wake up Dad, but loud enough to tell me my time was over.

"Hurry up!" she hissed.

I looked back into the mirror. Dark circles were nestled under my gray eyes. I ran the faucet until the water was frigid and splashed it on my face.

"Hurry up!" Trina spat again.

I combed my hair with more strokes than needed, pulled on a robe, hung up the towel and finally opened the door as slowly as I could. Trina pushed past without a word and shoved the bathroom door shut, narrowly missing catching my hair.

"Good morning, Rowan." It was my mom, awake, her voice wheezy and tired. She was sitting in the kitchen.

"Mom?" I squinted to make sure it was really her and not an illusion. "Um, I'll be there in a minute." I went into my room and pulled out a pair of faded jeans, grabbed one of my many long-sleeved T-shirts and a blue hoodie that had the word Army across the back in large, white letters. That was my staple wardrobe and I never, ever changed it. Even when the weather was ninety degrees and so humid you could melt like butter. I grabbed my backpack and headed toward the kitchen.

Mom sat at the small, round table with a cup of coffee untouched in front of her. There was a bruise along the right side of her face, barely noticeable with the way she wore her hair–pulled around her features like she was peering through a curtain.

"How'd you sleep, darling?"

"Fine. You?" I poured a glass of orange juice and put a piece of bread in the toaster. Every few seconds I glanced at her, but she just stared into the coffee cup and didn't answer my question.

"What's new with school?"

I popped the bread out of the toaster, trying to remember the last time we'd talked about school. That was probably when I was in the fifth grade–the second time I was in the fifth grade. Did she want me to go all the way back to the sixth grade and catch her up? I shook my head. "Nothing." I spread butter then jelly on the toast.

She laughed, a forced, lifeless sound. I winced as she continued, "I remember I used to say the same thing to Gran when she asked me that question."

Oblivious to my narrowed stare, she talked on. "Every morning she would ask, *Darling, what's new with school?* And I always answered like you just did. *Nothing, Mom. Nothing at all.* Teenagers are all alike. So little to say. So little to share."

How much sugar had she already eaten? Mom had what could be considered the worst diet in the world. She would devour huge amounts of food, mostly junk, then go and lay in bed all day. Her doctors warned her. So did I. And Gran. She didn't listen.

"But I always loved to talk to Grandma late at night, after she'd already gone to bed." She cupped the coffee mug between her hands. "I'd go in and wake her up to talk about boys…and friends…and boys. Mostly about your dad." Her laugh sounded nervous, forced.

She caught me watching her and turned toward the window, a faint blush coloring her cheeks.

"Gotta go, Mom." I kissed the top of her head, her hair leaving an oily residue on my lips. She needed a shower.

"You okay, Mom?" I threw the half-eaten toast in the trash.

"I'm fine. Fine." She chewed on her stubby fingernail.

"It's going to be a nice day. Good day for a walk."

Mom was just an inch taller than me. But she had to outweigh me by at least one hundred pounds. Maybe more. Likely more.

She finally put the cup to her lips and didn't bother to answer.

"Tell Trina I'll wait outside." I darted out the door.

It was thirty more minutes before Trina was ready, all perfumed, teased and puffed to perfection. She didn't speak to me as I left Levi's side and met her at the car. We were going to be late again. Another tardy slip for the Slone girls.

THERE WAS one parking space left in the school's lot and it happened to be beside Mike Anderson's blue sedan. He was late too, it seemed. He watched us pull into the empty space and for one brief moment our eyes met. I slammed on the brakes before I hit the car parked in front me.

"Easy, Ro," snapped Trina.

I shoved the car into *park*.

"Oh, there's Mike! I'm sure he'll want to walk me to class." She jumped out.

With teeth clenched, I stuck my head into my backpack, searching for a key I actually held in my hand. I opened my palm and let it fall in between my notebooks. It took longer than necessary to *find it*, but watching Trina flirt with Mike was not a show I wanted to see. And the thought of hopping out of my car and being pulled into their conversation made me want to lose the orange juice I'd had as breakfast.

"Dammit, where are those keys?" I grasped the metal key ring then let it fall again.

"Walk me to class?" I heard Trina say. I envisioned her twirling a strand of hair around her finger and popping grape bubble gum. She probably did no such thing, but it matched the tone of her voice somehow.

"Um, sure. I guess." He sounded hesitant. Or was that wishful thinking? It took all of my restraint not to look at the expression on his face.

I stayed bent over my backpack long past the shrill clang of the tardy bell. Then I jumped out of the car, yanking at my backpack. But it was stuck on the emergency brake. I yanked harder and the side split open. Textbooks and notebooks spilled out.

"Dammit." I fell to my knees and started shoving them back inside.

"Hey. If we're going to be biology partners, you might need to be a little more organized."

"What?" I glanced over my shoulder. Mike stood behind me, his face lost in the bright sunshine. "Oh, right." I forced a chuckle, ignoring the skip of my heartbeat. "I'll work on that."

He gathered a few of my papers, holding them as I tried to fit everything back inside the bag. I jerked the zipper shut and took the papers from him. "Thanks." I stood, shielding my eyes with my hand.

"You're welcome."

"I gotta go." I swung the pack over my shoulder. "I'm late."

He laughed. "Yeah, me too."

"What happened to Trina?" There was more edge to my tone than I intended. "I mean, I thought you walked in with my sister. Did you forget something in your car?" I waved to my side. "Need to talk about tonight?"

He slipped a hand in his jeans' pocket. "Nah. I just saw that you were still out here so I wanted to come and see if you needed any help."

Maybe he *didn't* like Trina? *Please let him not like Trina.*

"Oh, thanks." I started toward the school and he fell in step beside me. "Um," I started, "does seven still work for tonight?"

Please say yes. Please say yes.

"Yep."

I bit my lip.

"Hey, I have soccer practice until six. Wanna grab a bite to eat and then go to the library?"

Grab a bite to eat? With him? I wasn't one to squeal but if there was a squeal moment this would be it.

"Yeah. That would be cool."

Was it okay to say 'cool'?

"Great." He didn't seem to notice. "Let's meet at Mario's at six thirty. I'll be all sweaty after practice and that'll give me time to shower."

"Sounds perfect." In fact, nothing had ever sounded so perfect.

We passed through the main doors and Mike stopped at his locker. "I'll see you in class later."

"Okay. Bye." I walked away, but after a few short strides, every single muscle in my body froze up. Was he watching me? Something told me he was.

Please let my feet walk in a straight line. Please.

"HI, MISS J."

"Sit down, please, Rowan." Tanya Johnson, my guidance counselor, pointed to a chair across from her wooden desk. She rustled through some papers, shuffled a few into a small, neat pile and handed them to me.

"What's this?"

"College information."

"For which one?" I flipped through them without looking up.

"For two. A community college and a state school. You'll have an easier time getting financial assistance."

"What are my chances?"

"Your chances are good." Her round, coffee-colored eyes were wide and watching.

"My grades are good." The fact that I had to repeat the fifth grade shouldn't even show up on my records.

Miss J. stared at me, unblinking, and I hated that. So, I looked around the room. The bookshelf to my right was full of school-related items: ACT, SAT, GRE, teenage pregnancy, how to spot abuse–substance and physical, eating disorders, girls who cut themselves.

"They *are* good." Miss J. nodded but didn't avert her gaze.

The book on teenage pregnancy showed a very young looking girl in a rocking chair. Her stomach protruded almost out to her knees and she was gazing down fondly, as if being a teen mom was the most ideal situation in the world.

"Rowan?"

"Hmm?"

"Rowan, there's something we need to talk about; something that I think can potentially disrupt your future more than anything else."

The muscles in my neck tightened.

"I know what happened when you were ten was difficult to overcome but you did."

"Why are we talking about *that?*" I glared at her.

She ignored me and continued, "You just need to make sure you keep up the grades and the attendance." She left her chair and moved in front of the bookshelf, blocking my view of the pregnant teen.

Her face drew level with mine. "Rowan, it wasn't your fault."

I jumped up and walked to the window. "When can I apply? Can I get early admittance? Go early? Maybe next year and skip my senior year?"

She leaned against the edge of the desk, her hips spreading wide, and crossed her feet at the ankles. "No. There won't be early admittance. And it's very important that you continue to make good grades; to show them how serious you are about furthering your education. You're still tardy far too often."

The window blinds were gray from years of accumulated grime. I ran a fingernail over one plastic row and left a long, narrow scratch down the middle of the dust. Outside was the football field. In autumn, every Friday night the stands were packed with people eager to see our championship team play. Trina was down there last season, with all the other cheerleaders; wearing her tight uniform with her perky hair and annoying, flashy smile.

"Rowan?"

Miss J.'s lips were pursed and her head was cocked to the side as if waiting for me to bend to exactly what she wanted. What she wanted was for me to finish high school and go on to college. She wanted me to make good grades in college so I could apply to veterinary school, where I could be surrounded by more animals than people.

But *I* wanted these things. She could never know how desperately I wanted them. That's why I stayed up late into the night, exhausted, but studying five minutes more. Why I forced myself to get out of bed in the morning, despite another sleepless night, to get to school, if not on time, at least by second period. I couldn't control the tardiness, though. Not when I had to wait for Trina. But getting an education was my way out. My only way out.

I walked to the door. "Thanks, Miss. J." I yanked it open.

"Rowan."

"Yeah?"

"Look at me."

I did, through the corner of my eye.

"It wasn't your fault. You never should've been left alone with an infant. You were only ten. It's time to leave that to the past so that you can have a future."

"I'm fine. Just fine." My heart threatened to stop working the way it did anytime the past was brought up. "I'm making the grades. Doing fine. Why are we talking about this?"

She stepped toward me. "You carry the past with you like it's a bag of heavy stones weighing you down. I can see the strain on your face every day. You have to move on or you won't be able to have a future."

I slammed the door on my way out.

chapter three

THE REST of the day passed in a haze, the way it did anytime my baby brother's death was brought up. I saw Mike in biology class, but the teacher had packed each moment from bell to bell with instructions on the report: how to choose an appropriate topic, how to effectively research that topic, how to write a paper within AP guidelines.

On the way out, he flashed a smile. "See you tonight."

I prayed that seven o'clock would come quickly.

BUT IT didn't come quickly enough because I had to go to work. I hadn't heard from Dan since I'd sent that text. Was I really going to consider dating him? My thirty-year-old boss? I'd only sent that text because I was upset.

Maybe there would be a lot of customers today. With the weather getting warmer, maybe people would come out to buy a used car. That should keep him occupied and too busy to needle me about a date.

As if God had answered my prayers, Dan was outside with someone when I pulled in. He and another man stood on opposite sides of a used red pick-up truck, the staple vehicle for working men in this area.

Dan waved, the sun shining off the bald spot on the top of his head.

I went inside and starting cleaning up the used paper cups that Dan drank from but never threw away. Then I wiped the countertop and organized the papers that he'd strewn all over the place.

Several minutes later, he and the customer strolled through the door.

"Rowan, you know Jay Stockwell?"

I glanced up. "Hi." I put the papers in the metal basket.

Jay, a guy about Dan's age, leaned his elbows against the newly wiped counter.

"Hey, Rowan. How's your sister?" Jay bared his stained and crooked teeth. I think it was meant to be a smile.

"Fine. Dan, should I get the paperwork?" I moved further down the counter.

"Jay? Are we good?" Dan asked.

Jay, still watching me, nodded. "Yep. We're good. I'll pay cash."

I went into Dan's small, personal office to get the papers. Dan followed me in. "You okay?"

"I'm fine, Dan." I eased away from him and grabbed several sheets of paper from the filing cabinet. "Here." I handed him what he needed for the sale, but he didn't leave. He put his hands on my shoulders and leaned into my ear.

"I can't wait to go out."

My teeth clenched.

"We'll have a blast." He dropped his hands but didn't move away.

Suddenly, he was overwhelming me. Too large, with his expanded waistline. Too interested, with his earnest grin. Too stifling with his touches and whispers.

"I have to get some air." I hurried to the door.

His brows rose and his eyes widened.

"I, um, have a ton of homework. A test. I have a test." He followed me out of his office and leaned on the counter across from Jay. "I'm just stressed about a test."

"What grade are you in now, Rowan?" Jay picked at dirt under one of his nails. "You're a junior? Senior?"

Jay used to work with my dad at the prison but was fired for smuggling marijuana to the prisoners. He came to the car lot at least once a week to chat with Dan.

Ignoring Jay's question, I looked at Dan. "I'll be back in a minute."

I walked outside and the sunshine hit my face, warming my skin. Within minutes, sweat broke out on my forehead. It would get hot soon and I'd be faced with questions about my wardrobe all over again. It seemed that wearing long-sleeved T-shirts year round was a crime.

My phone dinged a new text message, but I didn't check it. The sky was cloudless, a light, pure blue that was almost painful to look at, though more difficult to look away from. It was perfect, beautiful. Spanning as far as I could see.

It reminded me of something, but I wasn't sure what. It wasn't my mom or my dad. There was no perfection there, sometimes not even enough goodness. Nor was it my sister, or Gran.

Then I realized what it was. The sky reminded me of Aidan. My sweet baby brother was just like the sky. And his eyes were the exact same color as the blue overhead.

My baby brother died when I was ten and Trina was eight. Hours before he went to sleep and never woke up, Mom and Dad had gotten into a fight over her weight and overall laziness. A spring storm had been brewing since early evening, mirroring the tension circulating inside the house. The wind howled through the trees, making them dance in the darkness, and rain fell in sheets. The lights flickered off and on a couple of times.

"I'm done with this," Dad had said. "You're a worthless wife. I never should've married you. My dad was wrong to guilt me into it!" He stormed through the house yanking on his raincoat and grabbing his

boots. "I'm leaving. Pack the boy's stuff. I'm coming back tomorrow to get him. Then we're leaving. I'm tired of this shit."

My mom scurried behind him down the hallway, wrenching her hands over her enormous stomach. Her eyes, red and swollen, followed his every move. When Dad stomped out of the house, he slammed the door so hard the floor shook under my feet.

Mom didn't move, her mouth hung open. Her hands shook as she made little whimpering sounds.

When Aidan began to cry from his crib, Mom went down the hall. She lumbered heavily past his door, not even pausing at his wails, and went into her room. The door shut behind her. The lock turned.

Trina stared at the television, not moving, not blinking. I got off the couch and followed Mom. Stopping in the middle of the hall, I looked between Mom's closed door and Aidan's. His wails hurt my ears, not because of the volume, but because I hated to hear him upset. I went into the nursery. I rubbed his tummy and cooed in my softest voice. His little face was red and blotchy, tiny fists clenched and thrashing in the air.

He wouldn't settle so I stood on a stool, bent over the crib and picked him up. He was only two months old but solid as a little linebacker. I managed to pull him into my arms and step off the stool without much trouble. I carried him down the hall and laid him in Trina's lap.

"Hold him," I had instructed her. "I'm going to make a bottle."

Trina glanced at me through vacant eyes, as if she couldn't quite focus. I nodded toward Aidan. "Hold him."

Without responding, she wrapped her arms around him. I went into the kitchen and had a bottle warmed and ready within minutes. I was used to making him bottles.

I took him from Trina and went back into the nursery. Nestled in the rocking chair, I tried to sing a lullaby, making up the parts I didn't know. He slurped and gurgled as the milk spilled into his mouth.

Aidan was an angel. At least he looked like one. It was no wonder Dad loved him so much. It was impossible not to. There was no jealousy in my heart over how Dad felt about Aidan, because I felt it too.

He looked a lot like Trina, with blond curls that were just starting to form around his little round head, giving him the image of a halo. His eyes were blue, round, clear. With cheeks that were permanently stained red, he looked like a cherub from a Bible story.

As I held his bottle, he reached his little fat hand up and grasped one of my fingers. I cooed, sang to him; even laughed as the milk spilled out of his mouth and down his chin.

After his bottle, I burped and changed him, then laid him back in his bed. He made only one small whimper of protest. When I started singing again, his eyes grew heavy. There were no blankets in his bed and none nearby. But his hands and feet felt cold. The storm raged on outside, rattling the windows.

I went into the hall closet and pulled out the smallest blanket I could find. It wasn't a baby blanket but thicker and heavier. I wrapped him up, careful not to cover his face, not even covering his shoulders. I tucked the blanket under his arms and around his torso. His eyes drooped until they shut completely and he released a soft, satisfied sigh.

Taking care of my brother was so natural, easy. I loved doing it. I really did. That night, the bad feelings of my parents' fight were replaced by warmth in my heart. I could not have known that my baby brother would never wake back up. That I would be the last one to take care of him, hold him, see those light blue eyes. That I would become the one blamed for his death because I had put that blanket on him.

AS TEARS filled my eyes, I tried to tell myself to look away from the sky, to convince myself that it would do me no good to stare at something so beautiful. It would only break my heart a thousand times over. Hadn't it already been broken enough?

Without realizing it, I had lifted the sleeve of my shirt and was scratching at my left arm; the dozen red, angry marks old and healed but still vibrant against the paleness of my skin. With my fingernail

I traced each line, forged the years after Aidan's death–when Dad's dark, accusing glare followed me through the house; when Mom grew more fat and unkempt than ever; when Trina narrowed her eyes and spat, *I hate you* so softly I wasn't sure I heard it.

And now, with each line I traced, I put more and more pressure using the edge of my nail. The skin did not break, but the pain was sharp and the burden of my heart slightly less.

Then Dan yelled my name.

I jumped up and yanked my shirt sleeve down. I went inside without a word, grabbed my backpack and bolted out the door with the two men's eyes burning a hole in my back.

WHEN I went to school to pick up Trina from cheerleading practice, she wasn't with the rest of her squad. "Jennifer, do you know where Trina is?" I asked a sophomore from Spanish class.

"She was here a minute ago, but I'm not sure where she went." She started gathering her stuff.

I walked along the sideline, trying not to steal looks at the soccer team running sprints. A few cat-calls rang out, but I didn't know if they were for me or someone else.

I walked toward the concession stand, where the bathrooms were, hoping to find her there. "Trina? We've got to go." Dad didn't like when we were late. If we had to go out later in the evening, he usually didn't mind so much. But he knew we should be home from work and practice by six fifteen. And it was almost ten minutes after six.

I went around the side of the small brick building. Soft murmurs wafted through the air. "Trina, we've got to go. Dad will be home." Those words would do it. And they did. Trina popped around the corner, pulling her shirt down. A boy I recognized but didn't know followed behind with his hand on the back of her skirt.

"Let's go." I walked away.

Trina and the guy started laughing, talking so low I couldn't hear what they said.

Then someone shouted my name.

"Rowan!" Mike ran toward me. "Hey! See you soon?"

He skidded to a stop right before crashing into me. He bent over, hands on his knees, inhaling short bursts of air. He was wearing athletic shorts, a T-shirt, and knee-high socks that showed the outline of his shin guards. After a few moments, he stood up.

"Yeah. I have to take Trina home and then I'll be back."

Beads of sweat rolled down the side of his face and he wiped them away with the hem of his shirt, displaying the hard muscles of his stomach in perfect fashion.

"Cool. I'll shower up and meet you there."

Trina walked up, alone. She ran her hand through Mike's hair. He yanked his head away and Trina laughed, loud and clear. "Don't want me to mess your hair up?"

"I was talking to your sister, Trina."

My eyes widened at the same time hers narrowed. She took a step back and looked at me. "Dad's waiting, Ro. Let's go."

"I'll meet you at the car." I held out the keys.

She yanked them out of my hand and stormed off.

"Your sister is something else." He frowned.

My heart did three flips and I swallowed the giggle that threatened to escape. *Maybe he didn't like Trina. Did that mean he liked...* But I shut down those thoughts before they even formed.

"I'll see you there soon. I'm starving!" He rubbed his stomach.

"Me too." I don't know why I said that because I was no such thing.

He grabbed my hand. His was warm, slightly moist; much larger than mine. He squeezed it and then darted off. I pressed my palm against my chest and couldn't stop the smile that spread across my face. I watched his calves, round and muscular and taut, pump him back toward the team.

"Ro!" Trina yelled from the car. "Dad's gonna be mad." That was all it took to make me turn from watching Mike's backside and hurry to the car. There was a distinct flutter deep inside my chest, but I wouldn't let Trina know anything about it. I set my lips and ignored her sideways stare as I pulled out of the parking lot.

TRINA WAS silent the whole way home, bolting into the house before I even got out of the car.

I gave Levi a hug and tummy rubs, then walked inside, trying to decide if I needed to change or wear what I had on.

"Rowan?" Dad's deep baritone halted me mid-step. He was sitting in the chair in the living room. "How was school?"

It took several moments for the words to sink into my brain. I hadn't heard that type of question from him in forever. Probably not since the fifth grade. Maybe not ever. Why were he and Mom so concerned with me and school today?

"It was fine."

"I got a call today."

I closed my eyes and inhaled. There was music, volume turned low, coming from the kitchen. It sounded like classic country, which is the only thing Dad listened to. Hank Williams, Johnny Cash, Patsy Cline. I knew all their songs by heart. He listened to this music when he was in a good mood; well, a good mood for him. So the call must not have been a bad one.

"Who from?"

He stood. My hands clenched the hem of my shirt. His boots pounded against the hardwood floor, sending vibrations all the way up my calves. Stopping in front of me, I could feel his hot breath on the top of my head.

"The school."

His name tag read *Jack Slone, Corrections Officer* written in black block letters deeply imbedded within a solid white background. It stood out against the somber gray of his uniform.

"Do you want to know what they wanted?"

I nodded against my better judgment.

"To tell me that you and Trina have been tardy twenty-five times this year."

A tiny bead of sweat rolled down my back.

He grabbed my chin with his strong fingers; fingers that fired guns and wielded police batons.

"Look at me, Rowan."

I did.

His eyes, hazel with red veins snaking through the white, stared down at me. I tried not to blink. He raised his other hand and I winced. Dad had never hit me, but there was an undercurrent of *something* that pulsed through him and made my knees knock together each time he got angry.

"I don't want another tardy slip the rest of this year." He ran the hand through his closely-cropped hair.

He released my chin and walked into the kitchen. I darted to my bedroom and shut the door. With shaking fingers, I yanked a brush through my hair and since it was already six thirty, I didn't bother to change.

chapter four

MARIO'S PIZZA was a tiny sliver of a restaurant, owned by one of the few immigrants in our rural area. Mario was from Sicily and had come here when he was twenty-one. He was now old, with two grown boys who also worked in the restaurant.

The restaurant was nestled at the end of a strip of local shops: post office, pharmacy, the used bookstore where Jess worked. I parked along the side of the building. Mike's car wasn't there yet and I didn't know if I should go in and get a table or sit in the car and wait. If I waited, I didn't want to look like I was waiting. So I flipped open my phone and texted Jess.

> Guess where I am?
> Where??
> Marios. Guess who I'm mtg?

I HAD just started to type the *M*, when I glanced at the clock. It was six forty. Where was Mike?

I didn't finish the text. Instead I replayed each and every discussion we'd had about meeting. He'd confirmed on the field, just an hour ago, and earlier in class. It was his idea to meet for pizza. Did he change his mind?

I wrapped my arms around my stomach and hurled the phone into my bag.

Maybe I should go inside and check. I didn't want him to think I stood him up. But then, if he wasn't there, wouldn't I look stupid if I turned around and left?

I chewed my fingernail as an SUV pulled into the next space. Before whoever was inside got out, I bent my head and rummaged through my bag until I found my phone again. Just as I was reading Jess' string of angry texts, demanding to know who I was meeting, someone banged on my window.

Breathing a sigh of relief, I glanced up with a smile. But it wasn't Mike. It was Trina, smirking. Beside her was the guy from earlier. My heart tumbled to my feet. Ignoring the sirens screaming in my ears, I rolled down the window.

"What are you doing out here all by yourself, Ro? Waiting on someone to come and pay you some attention?"

The guy had his arm around her shoulder, fingers grazing the top of her chest.

"No, Trina. For your information," and I wanted to *not* say the next words, because...what if he didn't show? But I just couldn't stop myself. "I'm meeting Mike. Mike Anderson." I also couldn't stop the satisfaction that spread across my face at her reaction.

Her lips pinched together and for the slightest of seconds, her expression flashed anger. But then it was gone like it was never there. "Oh, sure. You're supposed to study tonight, right? God, Ro. Get a life." Her laughter rang out over the parking lot as she sauntered into Mario's, the guy trailing behind like a love-sick puppy.

I slunk down in my seat. For all of the times to be stood up, why did it have to be in front of Trina? My bottom lip quivered as I started my car. I had to face the facts. He wasn't coming.

Then someone pounded on my window again. I almost didn't look up. If it was Trina again, I'd just die right there.

But I did look up.

And it was Mike Anderson.

RELIEF WASHED over me like a warm, spring rain. Not wanting him to see the moisture in my eyes, I blinked several times then rolled down the window.

"Rowan, I'm so sorry! I was on my way, but Coach wanted to talk to me about scholarships." Words tumbled out of his mouth. "Do you want to just go to the library?"

Trina was inside the restaurant with her date-of-the-moment. If I went in with Mike, it was hard to tell what her reaction would be. She could ignore us. Or diss her current date and come on to Mike again. Or she could say something embarrassing and hateful.

"I'm good. Let's go to the library. Unless you're hungry."

"Nah, I can't eat. Not now. Coach says I may get a scholarship to play soccer. Two colleges are interested."

"That's great." I forced my words to sound excited, though I couldn't understand in the least how it must feel to be so good at something that colleges fought over you.

Tonight Mike wore jeans and a yellow soccer jersey that had Brasil emblazoned across the front; both items of clothing falling *just right* over his body.

"So, let's go to the library. I'll follow you in my car."

I nodded, casting one last glance at the restaurant. I got to spend an evening with Mike Anderson. It didn't matter where or how. So take that, Trina.

THE LIBRARY was empty, quiet in the way only large, book-filled rooms can be. Mrs. Grey, our pinch-faced librarian, scrutinized my library pass through her glasses as if she hadn't seen it a hundred times over the years. Finally she thrust it back at me and settled into her desk chair. Mike followed me toward the end of the rectangular room, past cubicles with ancient desktop computers, past ceiling-high bookshelves.

We threw our bags down on a wooden table, its surface carved and colored as a testament to high school life: a misshapen heart with *Katie and Brian* etched inside, various scribbles, and a few unfortunate although funny remarks about Mrs. Grey.

Mike pulled out his biology book and it landed with a *thud* on the table. His notebook followed. He sat then looked at me with brows raised. "You okay?"

"Oh…yeah." I didn't realize I was staring at him. No, *studying* him. And he'd just caught me doing it. I fell into the seat beside him and bent down to get my things, and to hide my blush. There was something about this guy; his energy field engulfed everything around him, including me. Being near him made my skin actually tingle, and my head turn into a mass of idiocy.

"Where should we start?" He tapped his pencil against the table. "Believe it or not, I've tried to think of topics, but I can't. Science isn't really my thing."

What *was* his thing?

I cleared my throat. "I've thought of a couple. Here." I slid a sheet of paper over.

He scanned the sheet. "I like this one." He pushed the paper back to me with his finger on *Effects of Global Warming on the Intensity of Hurricane Activity*. "My mom is all about global warming these days. She thinks it's a sign that God is angry with us."

"Huh." *God?* "Sure. I guess that could be the case. I don't know. I don't really go to church."

"Man, I do. Every Sunday. My parents aren't fanatics," he said, opening his notebook to a clean sheet of paper. "But my mom, you know, was raised in the South, and has always gone to church. She volunteers there all the time-at the food bank, Walks for Veterans, mentoring kids. Things like that." He wrote our topic across the top of the paper.

Between me and Jess, it was hard to believe there *were* healthy, normal families; families that loved each other and loved spending time together; families that led you to talk about them with familiarity and love.

It was as foreign to me as the language Mario spoke when he talked to his sons at the restaurant. Jess would have felt the same way. Her mom left when she was two and her dad loved booze more than her.

"So," Mike went on, oblivious to my silence, "where do we start? I'm afraid you're going to have to take the reins on this. I mean, I won't leave you hanging with all the work." He put his hand on my knee and I jumped. He laughed, but didn't move it. "But I'll need some guidance."

I swallowed hard. "Um, sure. No problem. I've written a ton of research papers, so it shouldn't be a problem." I wrote the topic across my clean sheet of paper just like he had done. His handwriting was scratchy and ill-formed, like he couldn't be bothered. Mine was a testament to handwriting lessons in the second grade.

For the next two hours, we talked about where and how to research the topic. Even though he said he wasn't good at biology, he had good suggestions—like how to incorporate the religion angle. He even mentioned using his dad's friend who had a PhD in some environmental science, though he couldn't remember which one.

Before I knew it, Mrs. Grey was popping around the corner, coming at us as silent as a mouse. "It's nine o'clock, students. Time to go." With a cluck of her tongue, she walked away, her thin, bony shoulders pushing like points against her somber sweater. After she passed beyond the bookshelves, Mike and I glanced at each other; both with brows raised and started laughing.

"Boy, she's a load of fun, isn't she?"

"Shhh!" I swatted his arm, something I had never done. I had never been so at ease with someone to do something like that. Ever. "I have another year of school, don't forget. I need this library pass!"

Mike pulled his features into Mrs. Grey's sour expression and I laughed until I hiccupped.

"Stop!" My cheeks were starting to hurt.

"Okay. Okay. We'd better go before Ms. What's-Her-Name comes back here."

"Okay." I loaded my backpack. "Let's go."

Mike walked me to my car. It was a cloudless night, illuminated by a bright moon and hundreds of stars. Several streetlights lined the parking lot but only half worked, leaving my car cast in semi-darkness.

Mike and I faced each other, silently. He towered over me but instead of making me feel insignificant, I felt unique, special somehow. Wind blew through my hair, leaving several strands across my face. Mike, with the touch of a feather, tucked them behind my ear.

He bent down...and kissed my cheek.

Then he was gone.

EARLY THE next morning, I went outside while the house was still quiet. I'd gotten a few hours of sleep after staying up half the night studying for a chemistry test.

Levi awoke at the sound of my footsteps and walked toward me on sleepy legs. I sat beside him on the dew-kissed grass. Fog swirled around me, obscuring the mountain peaks that hovered in the distance.

Digging my hand into Levi's soft fur, I leaned into his solid body, feeling his warmth and the strong beat of his heart. The land lay still and peaceful around me. I breathed deeply, letting the crisp, fresh air fill my lungs.

It would be hard to leave this area after I graduated, not because of my family, but because of the beauty. This had to be one of the most beautiful places on earth. Unfortunately, within this beauty lived dark, somber people, living dark, somber lives. If my family were different and more like Mike's, I might actually consider staying close—instead of moving far away the first chance I got. I really would miss those mountains.

Maybe I could go to college in the northwest. I'd seen pictures and, though different, it seemed like a place I could call home. Lost in my thoughts, I almost didn't see the animal peering around the side of my car's tire. It was a kitten.

"Hello, little one." I eased my hand out. Two round gray eyes stared at me; wide, fearful. "I won't hurt you."

Levi stayed by my side, his big face turned toward the kitten, curious but uninspired to do anything about it.

"Come here, little friend."

Two ears popped into view.

"Come on."

I leaned forward and the tip of my middle finger met the moist pink nose. A sandpaper tongue licked my skin.

"Ew." I laughed. "Where did you come from? Are you hurt?"

Its head moved into full view, showing gray fur with weaving lines of white. It was tiny. It should probably still be with its mother. I scooped it up in one hand and it wrapped its little paws around my fingers.

"Hello, there" I held its face level with mine. It meowed softly. Pushing to my feet, I walked around the house then around the tree line, looking for its mother.

But there was no sign of a cat or any other kittens. Did someone drop it off on our property? That didn't make much sense, though neither did finding a motherless kitten. I snuggled it into my shirt, against the warmth of my chest, and nuzzled its downy head. It mewed softly and licked my chin. I kept my giggle quiet.

When the front door slammed, I turned expecting Trina, but instead saw my father. He spotted me before I had a chance to ease behind the house.

"Rowan?"

I hunched, trying to obscure the kitten. "Hi."

"Where's Trina? Don't you girls need to be getting to school? Remember what I said about those tardy slips." His voice was hard, the kind of voice you didn't talk back to.

"Yes, sir. She'll be here any minute."

I must've clutched the kitten too tight because it started to claw its way out of my shirt. Its little gray head popped out before I could turn away. Dad stared at me and then at the kitten.

"What's this?" he asked as I settled the animal with gentle strokes. Levi sat on his haunches behind me. He made no move to greet my dad.

"It was behind the tire of my car. I can't find its mother."

"I see. What do you plan to do with it?"

I shrugged. "Take it to the vet? Put an ad up at the grocery store?" What did he think I should do? A loaded question lingered somewhere in his words; I just wasn't sure where.

"Would you like to keep it?"

My eyes shot up and my mouth fell open before I could temper my reaction. "Keep it?" I blurted. "You mean I can keep it?"

He stared at the kitten, lips pulled tight. "It's asleep. You're good with animals." That was the biggest compliment he had ever given me.

I rubbed its head with my finger, cradling its back with the palm of my hand. It wasn't his nature to tease me though I couldn't help but wonder what he meant by his words. Conversations were rare in our household, and when they did occur, they hovered between uncomfortable and hostile.

"You and Trina could use a kitten."

I didn't blink for several seconds. He didn't touch the kitten, but his expression was less guarded than usual, and if not content, at least not full of anger.

"We'd—"

Before I finished, he was already heading toward his truck. His gray uniform shirt was clean, pressed to perfection, and his black boots were shiny like he'd slathered them in Vaseline. His walk was straight and proud, steps landing against the ground in confident thuds. He left without another word.

I darted into the house. "Trina!"

I skidded to a stop when I saw Mom sitting at the kitchen table. She was out of bed two days in a row. A miracle. Trina leaned against a counter eating yogurt from a plastic cup.

"What is it, honey?" Mom's breath came in rasps every time she inhaled. She was so overweight she was considered morbidly obese by her doctors. The extra weight put strain on her lungs, making it difficult to breathe.

I pulled the kitten out of my shirt. Trina squealed and the kitten jumped. She didn't try to take it from me, but pet its head as it snuggled into my shoulder.

"I saw Dad outside." Mom watched me, unblinking.

I nodded. "He saw it. He said we could keep it!" I bounced on my feet. "Mom, can you watch it today? We have to go or we'll be late again. I can take it to the vet later. I have money saved." I turned the kitten's face toward her. How could she resist?

Mom's smile didn't reach her eyes. She was probably worrying that it would interfere with her nap.

"Just give it a little milk?" I thrust it in front of her. Surely she couldn't resist that beautiful face. "Please, Mom?"

Finally she nodded. "Get a bowl and set out some milk. I'll watch it today. I can put together a litter box until you get to the store. You can't be late for school again."

I threw an arm around her shoulders. "Thank you!" I turned to my sister. "Trina, we have a kitten!"

My sister cracked a smile and I handed the kitten to Mom, who let it nestle into her terry-cloth robe. Trina and I darted out the door, talking about names, where the kitten would sleep, shifts of caretaking. We even made it to school on time. It was the best morning I could remember.

chapter five

JESS JUMPED off the school bus and snarled, "I hate that thing." She flicked imaginary dust off her black shirt. Ahead of us, Trina strutted up the stairs, acting like it was her own personal runway.

"Oh, guess what!" I exclaimed. "I found a kitten!"

"What? Where?" Jess pushed her glasses up her nose.

"Outside the house. I found it under my car's tire!"

"Wait." She pulled me to a stop. "Does your dad know?"

I snorted. Jess had met Dad once and that was enough. I didn't have her over to my house, even though that's what best friends do. Just like I rarely went to the apartment she shared with her father. We each had our reasons to keep people at a distance. For me, it was my obese, lazy mom and angry, resentful dad. For her, it was the fact that her dad was a raging alcoholic; not a violent drunk, but rather an insatiable drinker who preferred the stupor effect of large amounts of brown liquid and red wine to the harsh confines of reality.

"Believe it or not, he does. He even said I could keep it."

"Wow. What did you put in his coffee? Prozac?"

"Ha. That's funny. I'm saving that for Trina."

"Yeah. She's a real bitch."

"Hey! That's my sister you're talking about."

It was Jess' turn to snort.

"How are things with Paul?" I forced myself to ask because I knew it would make her happy.

Jess fanned her face. With a breathy sigh, she said, "Wonderful. We kissed." Her brows rose up and down.

I laughed. "How was it?"

"Oh, girl. He is a *great* kisser."

"That's a plus."

"You have no idea." She fell into my shoulder giggling and I couldn't help but giggle with her.

She wove her arm through mine. "I may even see if he'll take me to Prom."

"What? You can't do that! He used to be a teacher here!"

She flipped her dyed-red hair over her shoulder. "He's not anymore!"

"True." I didn't bother to ask what her father thought about her dating an older man. He was so oblivious, he would never notice if it wasn't pointed out to him. Even then, he probably wouldn't care as long as it didn't cause him any trouble.

She chattered on about the things Paul said on the phone last night, but for me, visions of Mike flittered through my mind, complete with me in a beautiful dress and perfectly coiffed hair and him in a black tuxedo. My arm would be curled through his as we strolled into the gymnasium for Prom. We would smile as we headed to the dance floor, where the melody of some soft ballad or another wafted from the speakers. He would hold me close, resting his head on top of mine. I would inhale the musky scent of his cologne. We would kiss…

I fell into a coughing fit, choking on saliva and images, neither of which I could control.

"Whoa." Jess hit me on the back. "You okay?"

"Fine. Just fine," I managed and we walked into the school.

AFTER WORK, I flew home to get the kitten. Trina had a cheer-leading meeting after practice so I didn't have to worry about her. She said someone else would bring her home. As long as it wasn't Mike, I didn't care.

Mom and the kitten were asleep in her bed. I slid my hand under the animal's warm body, careful not to wake up my mom, and grasped it to my chest. Then I drove to the vet's office.

It was crowded tonight. I signed in at the counter then eased into a seat beside an overweight woman with an animal carrier in her lap. A black cat's head pressed against the metal wire door, peering at me from huge green eyes. The kitten was tucked safely in my backpack.

I kept my eyes on the tile floor scanning the shoes of everyone in the waiting room. Gray Converse, black heels, brown loafers, black heels, red flats, what looked like steel-toed boots that I would've given my right hand for, two pairs of white tennis shoes, and one pair of blue tennis shoes that were covered with wisps of grass and a splattering of dirt.

My eyes traveled from the blue shoes to a pair of strong legs, rounded at the calves. The legs led to black athletic shorts and a DC United soccer shirt, worn and faded. Finally, my eyes landed on the owner of these legs and athletic clothes. It was Mike, his green eyes watching me.

He was sitting in a row of seats across from me, several people down. He smiled.

I smiled back, then dropped my eyes to check on the kitten, letting my hair fall over my face.

"Mrs. Jones?" called the lady behind the counter.

"Here." The woman beside me scooted her ample body forward until she managed to stand up, carrier handle secure in her mani-cured, plump fingers. She lumbered forward with a slight limp and a definite waddle. One pair of black heels gone.

One pair of dirty tennis shoes took their place.

"Here for a check-up?" Mike leaned into my shoulder.

"Excuse me?"

When he spoke, puffs of minty breath brushed against my cheek and I felt tingles in places I didn't even know could tingle.

"Are you here for a check-up?" He chuckled. "I don't see any animal." He waved his hand over my sitting body. "You have a dog, right? Is he in the back?"

"I found a kitten." I pulled apart the opening in my backpack.

He peered inside. "He's a little guy, isn't he?"

"Yeah. I found him this morning under the car. I couldn't find his mother."

"Wow." He reached a finger inside the pack and the kitten touched it with his nose. "Are you going to keep it?"

My stomach knotted as I watched his large hand gently pet the kitten. It purred and rubbed its head across his skin. "Yeah. My dad said we could keep it."

"That's really cool." He leaned back in his seat and looked around the room. His hair was wet like he'd just showered.

"Where's your dog?" Mike had a bulldog named Delilah.

"She's in back. Had to bring her in for a check-up. They're giving her shots now."

I nodded, watching the kitten swat at a string dangling from the zipper.

"Does it have a name?"

"Not yet. I only found it this morning. I don't know if it's a boy or a girl."

"Mr. Anderson?" called the lady at the counter.

"Coming." He took a few steps forward before turning back to me. "Hey. There was something I wanted to ask you."

A pair of white flip flops took Mike's old seat.

Before he could say more, Delilah darted into the waiting room, escaping captivity and the confines of a leash. She raced toward Mike as squeals erupted from the owners of all those shoes.

"Delilah," scolded the vet tech, scurrying after her. "Delilah!"

But Delilah had already found Mike and had her big front paws on Mike's thighs. He bent down and she covered his face with sloppy wet kisses. The kitten retreated to the dark corner of the backpack and I hugged it to my chest.

"Mike?" I wanted to know what his question was. I *really* wanted to know. And I *really* hoped it had nothing to do with our report. But then a lady squealed when Delilah swiped her wet tongue across her silk blouse.

Mike caught Delilah by the collar. "Delilah, down! Bad girl." He flashed a smile. "I'm very sorry, ma'am." My knees weakened, though I couldn't tell if he had the same effect on the lady. Delilah's tongue hung out of lips that looked like they were pulled into a mischievous smile. I giggled but cut it short when the lady threw me a nasty look.

"I'll call you later." He held tight to Delilah who was struggling to get back to the woman. The woman was grumbling and wiping at her shirt.

"It's going to stain...or stink...or both," she said.

"I'm happy to pay the dry cleaning bill." Mike flashed another smile.

She ignored him and he turned toward me.

"Did you need to ask me something? Do you, uh, have a question about our report?"

Please say no. Please say no.

His brows pursed as he considered my question. "No." He shook his head.

Yes!

He scooped Delilah into his arms. She covered his face with even more kisses. Lucky dog. "No, I didn't want to ask you anything about class."

"Then what did you want to ask me?" I clenched my teeth together. I didn't want to sound pushy, and sitting in a vet's waiting room with a crowd of people was not where I wanted to have the conversation I hoped we were having, but I couldn't help myself.

Getting to keep the kitten was already making this one of the best days of my life. What if…

"Miss Slone?" I glanced over, hoping to steal one more minute, but the receptionist was staring straight at me.

I stood, bringing me to Mike's shoulder. His question would just have to wait.

"I guess I'm being summoned. Do you, um, have my number?"

"Yeah. I got it from Trina."

My eyes widened. "From Trina?" I'm sure that conversation went well.

Mike laughed, but Delilah squirmed her way out of his grasp, jumped to the floor, and trotted around the waiting room toward a man who held a wide-eyed cat in his arms.

"Gotta go before I get sued." He darted toward Delilah and caught her just as the cat hissed. "I'll give you a call," he said over his shoulder and dragged his dog out the door. I swear I could hear Delilah's laugh echoing off the tiled floor.

A swift and painful bite to my lip stopped the smile that threatened to stretch right across my face to show everyone in the room just how much that boy affected me.

THE KITTEN, a girl, was given a full check-up and a clean bill of health. I stopped by the grocery store on my way home to get litter, a litter box, toys, and food. Then I thought about the empty refrigerator and picked up orange juice, a gallon of milk, apples, bread and peanut butter. Dad had given me a credit card for household errands. There was a low limit on it, but I managed with coupons.

After paying, I sped home actually excited to see my family. We had a kitten! I could see it now: the four of us sitting in our small family room, huddled over the kitten as it played with a small ball. We were laughing, even Mom, who was out of bed, showered, and dressed. Dad was also laughing, breaking out into a rendition of

"Isn't She Lovely" while our kitten jumped and batted at the toy. Trina's face, free of heavy makeup, was bright and beautiful, smiling and showing off the straight teeth that two years of braces had given her.

But when I pulled into our yard, Dad's truck wasn't there, and Gran's was. Bounding up the stairs, I shoved open the door.

"Gran?"

"Here, honey." She walked out of the kitchen, wiping her hands on a dish towel. "Shhh." She lifted her finger to her lips.

"Why?" I narrowed my eyes, scanning the family room and kitchen.

"Your mom's asleep." She motioned down the hall.

"Okay...she's always asleep. Why is today any different?" I usually wasn't rude to Gran, but if Mom was in bed that meant she wouldn't be a participant in my daydream.

Gran walked back into the kitchen without responding.

"I found a kitten and Dad said we could keep it." The kitten tumbled out of my backpack and skidded across the faded tile floor. "See?"

She glanced over her shoulder. "Oh, it's cute!" She turned back to the stove and stirred something that smelled like cream, spices and chicken. My stomach grumbled. Another day had passed by and I still hadn't eaten much. That was why I was so thin, and I knew it. Food didn't always sit well with me, though. At least it hadn't the past seven years.

I fell into the kitchen chair just as she set a steaming bowl in front of me. It was chicken and dumplings. My mouth watered and I grabbed a fork.

"How's school?"

"Good." I shoved a bite into my mouth.

"You're still making good grades? On track to graduate next year?" Her back was to me as she ladled food onto another plate.

"I've been back on track. Why?" The food turned hard in my mouth.

"Just asking." Her tone was vague, full of hidden meanings and unasked questions.

She put a cup of water down in front of me. I gulped it to try and moisten the ball of food. I choked as I forced myself to swallow. The food, at first bite delicious, was stale and plain now; the smell suddenly offensive.

Gran refilled my water, watching me from behind heavy lids. I frowned back at her, not trying to hide the irritation that was growing inside of me. I hated these *how are you coping* talks. There had been countless over the years. They were always the same and they were always unhelpful.

"How's your mom been?"

I let the fork fall into the bowl with a loud clang. "What's going on? Gran, why are you here?"

With a sigh, she pulled out a chair and sat down; the bowl of dumplings in front of her untouched. With fingers forked under her chin she stared at the table and then wiped away non-existent crumbs.

"Your mom is in bed again. She's been there since you left for school."

"You've been here all day?" I looked around. The house *was* clean. Gran did that every now and then; showed up to clean, do laundry and cook while Mom, as was typical, spent the day in bed. There was nothing unusual here.

"Yes. I got here right after you left for school."

"She stays in bed every day." The knots in my stomach started to unroll. This conversation was no big deal. Just a regular check-in to see how life at the Slone house was flowing along. I put a piece of chicken into my mouth, judging the taste. It was creamy again, flavorful and mouth-watering.

I had another bite ready as Gran continued, "So she's still doing that every day? Staying in bed?"

I shrugged. "She's been out of bed a little bit more, I guess."

"Rowan?"

I looked up, wiping my mouth on a napkin. "What?"

"How are things around here?"

"Things are fine," I answered, visions of the four of us playing with the kitten fresh in my mind. I shoved in another forkful of food.

"Rowan."

"What? Quit saying my name!" I demanded. Couldn't she just be quiet? Nothing in this house had changed. Nothing ever would.

I pulled the kitten, meowing by my feet, to my chest and nuzzled it against my face; letting her nearness take the entire focus of my mind. Her fur smelled dirty but sweet. I'd give her a bath in the sink after dinner. Then she could sleep in the bed with me, snuggled against my chest. Trina would lose interest in her and she'd be all mine. Maybe she could go to college with me. Maybe I could leave for college right now and avoid the rest of this conversation.

"Today is the anniversary of your brother's death."

I shoved the bowl away and scowled at the table. I didn't eat another bite.

chapter six

I HAD forgotten what today was. I shouldn't have, though. The somber, hopeless mood of this day wove its way into our souls and rested there like a black mass. Not moving. Not lessening. Each passing year made the mass a little bigger, a little deeper.

Seven years since Aidan died. Seven years since I became the daughter known as the one who put that blanket on him and caused him to die.

I grabbed my bag and went to my room without saying anything else. Gran knew there was nothing to say. She'd tried to help over the years, to tell me it wasn't my fault; to help my mom wake up from her stupor; to help deflect Dad's resentment toward me that always simmered behind every glance he cast my way. But there was no hope for us anymore.

My hand shook as I locked my door. I didn't have any of the things I'd bought at the store so I crawled out my window and darted to my car. I threw the bags through my window and crawled back inside. After peering down the hall to make sure it was empty, I darted to the kitchen, threw the things into the fridge then hurried back to my room.

I pushed my earphones into my ears and turned the volume up on the iPod I'd bought with money I'd earned from working. It was so loud, I almost couldn't stand it. But it made it impossible for any thoughts to take root.

Several minutes passed and with each pounding note, my mind released a little more of its hold on the pain. I rubbed my left arm with fingernails that needed to be cut, but I didn't pull up the sleeve of my shirt. I was determined not to go back there.

AN HOUR or so later while holding the kitten, which I named Scout, I cleaned out an area near my desk for the litter box. I set her down in the gravel and watched her watch me. Then I cleared space for food and water bowls near my closet door, putting an old ragged towel underneath so spills wouldn't hurt the floor. I'd give my dad no reason to change his mind about letting me keep her. In fact, I wouldn't even let her out of my room. Trina would forget about her, if she hadn't already. I'm sure Mom already had. And Dad would forget his gracious deed soon enough, if there were no traces of our new inhabitant.

While Scout explored her new home, I shut my window so she couldn't climb out and then fell back on my bed, suddenly exhausted. There was no escaping this day; no stopping the blackness that oozed through my body like oil. I tried not to think about Aidan's little face, how it looked in his peaceful sleep, or how it looked in his cold death. But the images flipped inside my mind anyway; with each new beat, a new picture appeared.

Soon my cheeks were wet and the hole in my heart ached with the ferocity of a tsunami. I wrapped my arms around my waist, trying to hold in my insides.

He was beautiful; sweet, so sweet. I turned up the volume so high my head pounded as flashes of chubby, pink cheeks and light blue eyes loomed in my mind. I slammed my fist into the pillow.

He was so cold that day, cheeks like cool marble. His hands were frigid. His feet, too. I could feel that coldness now as I thrashed in bed. I should never have put that blanket on him. I should've realized that there wasn't a blanket in his bed—in his room—for a reason.

The next morning, I woke up eager to see Aidan again; hoping I could give him his morning bottle. But when I opened his door, I saw that he was still asleep. There was a strange, unnatural color to his skin that pulled me forward, lured me to the crib's side. The blanket was still on him, covering his chest and the rest of his body. But he was blue, like he was really, really cold.

I shook his tummy. He didn't move. He felt cold. Stiff. Solid. I pushed again. Feelings I can't put into words bubbled up through my body. His lips were blue. His eyes steadfastly closed. I picked him up and held him tight to my chest, hoping my warmth would make him melt back into the baby he was last night.

Then I heard Dad's truck pull up in front of the house and the front door slammed shut behind him.

Mom bolted out of her room. She was still dressed in her clothes from the night before, a stained white T-shirt and cotton skirt.

"Let me have the baby, Ro," she'd said from the doorway to the nursery.

"I want to hold him, Mama." I turned my back to her. I didn't want her to see him. To know what I wasn't even sure I knew yet.

"Give him to me, Rowan." Her voice was urgent, heavy with fear and determination. I could hear Dad walking down the hall.

I clutched him closer. "No."

She shoved her fingers, strong and pudgy, between his body and mine. She pulled. I clutched him to me. She pulled harder. I held on tighter.

"Where's my boy?" Dad demanded. His voice was gruff and scratchy, like it often was when he drank.

My mom and I locked eyes. She broke away first and looked down at Aidan. I watched the wave of insanity tear its way into her eyes. It would nestle there, take root. After this day, her eyes would never return to normal—like her eyes before this day had never really existed.

"Amy, where's my boy?" His voice boomed and I envisioned the picture frames shaking on the walls. "Where's my—" He stopped. His eyes jumped from Mom, to me, to the baby in my arms.

"No!" he shouted.

The world went black.

My nose ran and my eyes burned. I rocked back and forth to the rhythm and the pain of the nightmares. Scout meowed by the bed, wanting up. I almost didn't hear her through my sobs.

I scooped her up, opened the window, and climbed outside. I stumbled to the woods, just out of reach of Levi's chain. I let Scout go.

I couldn't be trusted to care for the little kitten.

She meowed softly and jumped on my shoelace. I staggered back.

"Go. Go, Scout. I can't take care of you." I ran back to the house before she could follow and I cried myself to sleep.

"GET UP! Get out of that bed!"

I was on my feet before I even opened my eyes.

"Get out here!"

It was Dad.

I darted toward the window as he banged on my locked door. Then he kicked it with his boot. My body erupted in shivers. I watched the door shake under his foot, unable to move, unable to flee.

"Open this door now!"

"Jack, please!" screeched Mom.

"Open it!" he yelled.

"Daddy!" cried Trina.

"Shut up!" he shouted.

"Jack, I'm going to call the police." It was Gran. She was still here.

"Call anyone you want," he spat. "Rowan!"

My feet shuffled forward even though my mind screamed not to. I swung the door open then stumbled back to the window. Dad filled the space of the doorway, then stalked toward me.

"Did you know?" He grabbed me by the shirt and lifted me to my toes.

"Know what?" I rushed. "Mom? Mom, did I know what?" But she just hovered there, a sweater pulled tight over her large stomach.

Trina huddled in the hallway behind Mom, streams of black makeup running in parallel lines from her eyes down over her cheeks. She wouldn't look at me.

"Did you know that your sister is pregnant?" His tone was full of accusation, like I'd led her to have sex with my own hand.

I shook my head. "No. No, I didn't know. When? How?" I sputtered. Trina's pregnant? She was only fifteen!

Dad dropped my shirt and I stumbled away. Then he yanked Trina into the room, his hand an iron clamp around her arm.

"Jack," warned Gran.

He ignored her. "Rowan, when did your sister have a chance to get pregnant? Aren't you supposed to be looking out for her? She's fifteen, for God's sake. *Fifteen!*"

Mom turned away and shuffled down the hall.

The walls inched toward me, threatening to close in. "I picked her up every day I was supposed to. I only didn't if she had to stay late. And then she always found another ride and was home in the evening. I don't know." My palms were moist. I wrung them in the hem of my T-shirt.

"You." His words slammed into me like powerful punches. "You are responsible for this."

I stared at him then at Trina. He released her arm and she slid down the wall into a ball. There were no new tears on her cheeks but she was pale and looked nothing like a fifteen-year-old pregnant girl. Instead, she looked like the little sister whose hair I used to comb and whose nails I used to paint.

I didn't bother to ask Dad how I was responsible. Since that day seven years ago, I'd become the responsible party for every bad thing that happened to our family. It didn't even faze me anymore. At least I told myself it didn't, scratching my left arm like I was being bitten by fleas.

I could sense the strength waning from Dad as he watched me, like a balloon with a tiny pin-prick hole that allowed the air out so slowly you almost didn't notice. He'd found the one responsible. And now he'd tell me to fix it.

"Take her to get rid of it."

"Take her to get rid of it?" This is how I would *fix* it.

"Tomorrow. Your worthless mom can't do it." He stomped down the hall then the door slammed behind him. He started his car. The kitten!

Please don't let her be under his truck.

The truck's tires spun out on the dirt driveway, but then I heard the truck drive away and silence was all that was left.

"Trina?" I whispered.

She looked at me through empty eyes.

"Is it true?"

She didn't answer.

"How'd they find out?" I'm sure she wasn't broadcasting this news.

"Gran found the test in the trash."

"You didn't think to cover it up? Throw it away somewhere else?" Buy herself some time before someone found out?

"Yes, Ro," she spat. "I shoved it to the bottom of the trash. How would I know today Gran was going to come and clean? It's not like I wanted Dad to find out."

"Gran told him?"

"No," she huffed, as if my questions irritated her. "He overheard us talking about it."

Was she so careless to not try to keep this quiet? "Who...who's the father?"

Her eyes narrowed, flashing an emotion that I had never seen in her before, an emotion that sent a cold shiver across the back of my neck. "Mike. Mike Anderson." Then her head fell into her crossed arms and she didn't look back up.

I PULLED my old razor out from between my mattresses and ran my finger over the edge. It sliced through the skin. Small bubbles of blood formed and I squeezed. The cut was shallow, though, and didn't bleed freely. I wrapped a tissue around it.

Slipping out of my hoodie, I pulled up the sleeve of my T-shirt, exposing my left arm. Angry red slashes, healed wounds, ran in uneven lines up and down my arm. With a slow, deep breath, I focused on the cold steel between my fingers letting it become the only thing I could feel. I rested the razor against my skin. And cut.

Inhale. Exhale. The world slipped away.

chapter seven

I WIPED the razor blade clean with a tissue and slid it back under my mattress. I sat on the bed for several minutes, breathing in, breathing out, and letting the release ease into my mind and my heart.

Then I lifted the window and climbed out.

"Scout?" I called into the night. "Here kitty, kitty." It was dark, only a crescent moon and a cloudy sky overhead. A dim bulb illuminated the square, concrete porch but did little to light up the yard. "Levi, where did the kitty go? Have you seen her?" I stumbled around the side of the house. Levi bounded to my side and licked my hand.

"I...I accidentally let her go. I need to find her. Levi? Have you seen her?" I moved in a circle taking in the yard. Then I did it again. And again. I looked under my car. "Is she here, Levi? Did she go under here?"

At some point, I started to cry. Finding Scout was all that mattered now. Not Trina. Dad. Mom. Just Scout. If I didn't find her then I'd certainly failed at everything.

My arm throbbed. I had cut deeper than I meant to. Before when I cut, I knew how to apply the perfect amount of pressure. My steady fingers would slice straight line after straight line, deep enough for the calm to set in but no deeper. Now, I clutched my arm around my stomach and tried to ignore the throb.

"Scout?"

Gran walked onto the porch. "Rowan, who are you talking to? Are you okay?"

"Scout?" I walked around the side of the house. "Here, kitty, kitty. Scout? Time to eat."

I rested my hand on Levi's large head and called to the kitten over and over. But I didn't hear her. I didn't see her. I wouldn't be able to find her.

I collapsed to the ground. Wrapping my arms around Levi, I sobbed into his fur; sobbed for Aidan; for my broken family; for my lost sister and now my lost kitty. I sobbed for my lost maybe-almost-boyfriend, maybe-almost Prom date. Heaves wracked my body, but Levi didn't mind. He sat stoically, proudly; willing to be the raft that kept me afloat.

Then I heard it. The softest, tiniest meow. I sat up. "Scout?" I scanned the dark yard, wiping my face with the sleeve of my shirt. "Scout? Come here, baby. Come here."

And she did. She eased out from behind the shed.

"Come here, Scout."

She came right to me and dove for my laces. I laughed; one arm still secure around Levi's back.

"Hello, little one," I whispered, afraid she would run away, not trust me. But she just kept bouncing onto my laces, grabbing one within her tiny, white paws, then yanking on it until it slid away from her. Then she did it again. I forced a laugh. Tried to smile.

Then I couldn't resist and I picked her up, cuddling her close to my chest. The three of us snuggled together in the cold night.

"ROWAN?" GRAN sat on the ground. With her arm around my shoulders, she pulled me toward her. I didn't resist, but I did bring Scout and Levi with me until the three of us were practically sitting on her lap.

She stroked hair from my forehead and planted soft kisses on my head like she did when I was a small child.

"I'm okay, Gran," I muttered into the kitten's fur.

Gran was my mom's mother. She raised my mom and her two sons by herself after her husband died when my mom was a baby. When I was twelve, I tried to convince my parents to let me go and live with her but they wouldn't. Mom said she needed me around to help and that she'd miss me. Dad didn't say anything other than *no*.

"I must say, I'm not surprised." Gran's voice carried through the night. She looked up to the sky as if she could find the right words there. A wispy cloud passed over the moon. The stars, often so bright and abundant, were faded and stark.

"I tried to warn Amy but she wouldn't listen."

"Warn her about what?"

"That Trina was out of control."

"Did you think she'd end up pregnant? She's only fifteen." With the word, *pregnant* a vision of Mike worked its way down to my throat where it made the muscles constrict and nearly sever my breathing. Only by clenching my teeth and squeezing my eyes shut would the image float away. I refused to acknowledge the waves of nausea that threatened to make me vomit all over my animals. I simply was not that upset. I wasn't. And I wouldn't let myself be.

Gran pulled in a deep breath, held it, and then let it out slowly. "Just a hunch. She's been acting wild lately. And, you know, it's a small town. Word gets around."

I thought about the day I found Trina behind the bathroom with that boy; a boy that hadn't been Mike. Was it possible he wasn't the father?

"Do you know this boy she says is the father?"

The moon was just a slither of its full beauty. There was something unfulfilled about it tonight; like it was only a remnant of its former glory, afraid it would never achieve it again. It would, though.

The moon would regain its glory over and over. I didn't think any of us would. It slid out of sight behind another feathery cloud.

"I know who he is." I snorted. "He's my biology partner."

I refused to say his name. It went into a little box of *never open under any circumstances* that I kept in the back part of my brain. From now on, the father of Trina's baby would be a nameless, faceless boy who'd made a stupid mistake.

"His name is Mike? What's his last name?"

Her question threatened to force my freshly shut box to open and I jumped to my feet. "I dunno. I'm going out." I held the kitten in one hand and unleashed Levi.

"Where are you going, sweetheart?" She gazed at me with eyes that were full of a grandma's concern.

"I'll be back later. Relax. It's not like I'm going to get in trouble. Trina has taken the cake on that one."

And I walked off. Levi followed close on my heels. Opening the car door, I motioned for Levi to get in. He nestled himself into the passenger seat. I put the kitten on my lap, started the car, and took off down the road.

I didn't know where I was going; just knew I had to go somewhere. So I pulled over on the side of the road and flipped open my phone.

R u home? Is ur dad there?

I hit *send* to Jess' phone.

She responded immediately.

Yep. Dad's here with new gf. Fun. On their 2nd bottle of vino. U ok?

I didn't bother to answer, flipping through my other options. Maybe I could go to Dan's house. The thought made acid spring to my throat, but I didn't shut it away. It *was* a possibility. If I found nowhere else to go, I could go to him. He wouldn't turn me away.

Was there nowhere else I could go?

I OPENED the web browser on my phone and typed in *Tanya Johnson*. After a few minutes of searching, I found the address I wanted and pulled back onto the road.

I drove through town, past the car lot, the used bookstore and a handful of other businesses. Then I turned off Main Street and found the place I was looking for.

The apartment building looked more like a large house with pale wooden stairs winding up the outside. It was divided into six or so apartments. The one I wanted was on the first floor.

I parked the car and put Levi on his leash, slid Scout into my bag, and jumped onto the pavement. The place was deserted except for Miss J.'s beige station wagon plastered with all sorts of odd and strange stickers.

Before I changed my mind, I walked over and stopped in front of apartment 1A. The clouds had grown heavier blocking most of the moon's rays. But the parking lot had one lonely light that cast an eerie, yellow sheen over everything on this side of the building.

I knocked.

The sound of Miss J.'s voice filtered through the wooden door. She was chattering like there was someone in the apartment with her. I wanted to see *her*, not a friend or God forbid a boyfriend.

But when she opened the door, she held a phone to her ear.

"Rowan?"

I glanced down at Levi.

"I'll call you back," she said into the phone. "There is a student at my door." Her tone was dry, belying the bewildered expression on her face. "Rowan, what are you doing here? Is everything okay?"

"Trina's pregnant."

"What?" Her mouth fell open, revealing clean, white teeth. Miss J. was a pretty lady, with long, straight brown hair that she usually wore pulled back in a clip. Today it was on top of her head in a messy bun. She wore yoga pants and a sweatshirt with a college logo sprawled across the front. She had been my guidance counselor since the ninth grade.

"Yep. Preggers. Knocked-up. Bun in the oven."

She stared at me then looked at Levi. "Why are you here?"

With a shrug, I petted Levi's head. "Dad said it was my fault."

"That your sister got pregnant? How is that your fault?" After another shrug for an answer, she sighed. "You shouldn't be here."

Moisture filled my eyes, but I didn't look up. I felt the kitten tumbling around in my bag. "I have a kitten. Do you want to see it?"

"Here with you?"

"Yep." I pulled my bag from my shoulder and unzipped a small opening.

Miss J. peered inside. "Very cute." She didn't pet Scout and was quiet for a moment. "And who's this?" She did pet Levi's head and he licked her hand.

"Levi. My dog."

"I can see why you want to be a veterinarian."

I nodded.

"Rowan, did something happen at home? I need to know why you're here."

"Look," I snapped. "I didn't have anywhere else to go. But don't worry about it. I'll leave."

"Is everything okay at home? Did someone hit you? Hurt Trina?"

"No. Everyone's fine. See you later." I turned to go.

"Rowan, wait." Her hand grazed my arm. "It's not appropriate for you to be here. At my home. Do you understand that?"

"Got it. I'm leaving. You don't have to ask me again." I yanked my arm away.

"Except," she said, and her hand was back on my arm, "I can see you're upset. I'm not going to invite you in, however, that doesn't mean we can't chat for a couple of minutes. Let's sit on the stairs. But, Rowan, it has to be just this once. You can't come to my home again."

With a huff, I sat. I really didn't have anywhere else to go. Dan's, I guess. But I wasn't ready to go there.

Miss J. sat down beside me. She smelled nice, like scented lotion or something.

I pulled my hoodie sleeves over my hands, and then pulled Levi back to sit between my knees. His warmth soothed me. The kitten was quiet in the bag.

"I want to finish high school," I started. "Then go to college. I want to go to college then on to veterinary school. I want to be a veterinarian. Maybe a tech or something like that." I glanced up at her. "Do you think that's possible?"

She opened her mouth to respond, but I continued before she had a chance. "I can go to work for that old vet that'll be dead soon. The practice will need a new one. If the old guy can hang on until I'm ready then I'll take his place. You can call me Dr. Slone. Wouldn't that be cool?"

Her doe-like eyes watched me from beneath heavy brows. "Rowan, you can do anything you set your mind to. I truly believe that. If you want to finish high school and go to college, I see absolutely no reason why you can't make that happen. Your grades are good. Your attendance is good. You just need to quit being tardy so often."

I snorted. "Yeah. I only have so much control over that. Trina is the one that makes us late."

"I thought that might be the case."

I glanced at her but she was staring up at the sky. Her eyes almost didn't seem human. More animal-like, though not in a bad way. I wanted to ask her if she had a boyfriend.

"What did your parents say about Trina being pregnant?"

I shrugged.

Scout shimmied in the bag but I jostled it gently and she settled back down.

"How did your parents find out? Did she tell them?"

"Gran found the test. Dad walked in while Gran was talking to her."

Miss J. was quiet as she petted Levi on his head. He leaned toward her, resting his chin on her knee.

"Sweet dog you have here."

I nodded.

"Who's the father?" Her eyes fell on me. "Rowan?"

I scratched my arm, feeling the just-formed scab give way under my shirt.

"Mike Anderson."

"Mike Anderson? The soccer player?"

I nodded, then I stood up. "Guess I'd better go."

"Rowan? Are you okay?"

I sighed. "I'm fine." I *was* fine. I was just fine. "I guess I'd better get back."

She stood. Miss J. was only a couple of inches taller than me. Maybe even only one. She was far more voluptuous, but I could see where we resembled each other. More than Trina and I. Miss J. and I could be sisters. She could be my older sister, stealing home from late-night dates to tell me all the details while we sat cross-legged on her bed.

"Okay," Miss J. said finally. "Check in with me tomorrow at school. Okay? *At school.*"

"Yep." I darted toward the car with Levi on my heels, images of a different sister dancing in my head.

"Hey!" she called. "How did you do on that chem test?"

"Aced it." I jumped into the car. Before I slammed the door, I heard her say, *good girl.*

I drove back home because I didn't really have anywhere else to go.

chapter eight

DAD'S TRUCK was gone when I got home, which wasn't unusual. Anytime something happened in our home, whether it was a fight with Mom or he was aggravated with me or Trina, he left. He usually returned some time during the night.

I crawled in through my window after putting Levi on his leash. The house was quiet, the only remnant of the earlier drama a general unease that permeated the air. Or maybe it was just inside of me.

When I peeked out of my room all I found were closed doors. I crept to the bathroom, washed my face and brushed my teeth. Then I pulled a Band-Aid and ointment from the medicine cabinet. My new wound wasn't severe but it was ugly; red and slightly swollen, partly scabbed over and crusty.

My arm looked like a restaurant chopping block. I hadn't meant to start cutting again. I had gone years without reaching for the razor and I thought I was over it. If not the urge, at least the ability to control it. And I had been able to control it. Until now.

It was late. But I didn't want to sleep. Who knew what nightmares I'd have?

So I pulled out my trig book with thoughts of college...and escape...pushing me through the next several hours.

SUNLIGHT STREAMED through my opened curtains, burning through my closed lids. Scout licked my nose and when I opened an eye, her little face was staring at me.

"I know. I know. It's time to get up."

The clock read six. I had finally fallen asleep sometime after three and I didn't feel rested at all. Rather, I felt achy and weak. I wasn't sick, though. It was Trina's words, hanging around me like rabid dust mites, threatening to bite at me until there was nothing left.

Mike had gotten Trina pregnant. Pregnant. My fifteen-year-old sister was pregnant. By the boy who could've possibly, just maybe, asked me to the Prom.

Naïveté was not for me, but I really didn't see this one coming.

I put a fresh Band-Aid on my arm and bit the tips of my fingers to keep from reaching under my mattress and grabbing the thin, cold razor. Without bothering to comb my hair, I yanked on my clothes and stuffed my books into my backpack. Then I forced my feet to carry my body out of my room, where I found Gran standing in our kitchen.

"Hi, Gran. You're here early."

"I got here a few minutes ago." She turned to the stove. "Are you hungry?"

The smell of eggs and bacon made my stomach turn and not in a good way. "Sure." I sat down at the small table.

"I'm glad you're up. I wasn't sure what time you needed to leave for school."

"I have plenty of time. Is T-T-*she* up?" I choked on her name. Each time I thought of her now, I thought of Mike. Mike. Tall, dark, and handsome Mike. Senior in high school Mike. Mike who had held the door open for me when we went to the library. Mike who had gotten my sister pregnant.

How could I ever look at Trina the same again? Pass Mike in the halls?

My chest constricted into a weighty ball. We still had to work together on our biology report.

"I wouldn't worry about Trina," Gran said. "I think she can miss school today." She sliced large chunks of watermelon on a wooden board. Then she laid a plate, heavy with food, in front of me. I swallowed against the bile and closed my eyes, pulling up a vision of my ribs reflected at me in my bedroom mirror.

Today I had put on a belt to help hold up the jeans that always fit perfectly, even given me more of a butt than I really had. They didn't anymore, though. And my long-sleeved shirt, the essential staple of my meager wardrobe, hung on me like I was nothing more than a wire hanger in a department store's juniors' section.

No wonder Mike preferred my voluptuous sister.

I shoved a spoonful of eggs into my mouth, ignoring the scalding burn at the back of my throat.

"Slow down, Rowan. You're going to make yourself sick."

I devoured a piece of bacon.

"Rowan!"

"What?" I demanded, mouth full.

"Quit eating so fast!"

"I'm losing weight again. I'm too skinny."

She yanked the plate away from me mid-bite. "Eat like a civilized human being."

I took a swig of orange juice and motioned for her to return the plate, which she did. Then I slowly eased my fork down, scooped up the eggs and transferred the food to my mouth. It was far more difficult to eat this breakfast than I'd ever admit.

"How's that?" I tried to tone down the sarcasm.

Gran forced a smile, though it didn't reach her eyes. "Better. Are you trying to lose weight? You don't need to get any skinnier."

"Just busy. I *am* working and going to school, you know."

"Is that all?" Her hand went to her hip.

"Yes. That's all. I promise. I don't like when I get thin. I look like a skeleton."

"You don't look like a skeleton. But I don't want to see you getting skinnier. You'll have me to answer to if you do."

"Okay, okay." I shoved in another spoonful, choking it down. Then I jumped up, grabbed my bag and an apple that I would never eat, and went to the door. "Are you staying here today?"

"I'll clean up then head out."

I nodded and left. "Bye, boy," I called to Levi who sat along the side of the house, watching me. I hopped in the car and went to school.

THE FIRST warning bell clanged through the parking lot. My feet felt heavy as I started toward school. Mike was probably in there. He'd be in biology class later. There was a chance we'd have to pair off and work on our reports. Or the teacher would lecture the entire time—here's hoping—and there wouldn't be a minute to spare. If I was careful, I might be able to make it through the day without interacting with him.

But, standing at the bottom of the stairs, leaning against a guardrail, *was* Mike watching me walk toward the school. If my feet felt heavy a minute ago now they were concrete-laden bowling balls.

Mike and I were nothing, though. He owed me nothing. I was just a delusional little twit. Who was I to think he could like me as anything more than friends?

Since there was no other entrance, I heaved my bag over my shoulder and stomped ahead.

He pushed off the guardrail. "I need to talk to you." His features were hardened somehow, with none of the light teasing and flirty smile that was usually there.

I pushed past him, my vision blurred with rage and tears. "You must have mistaken me for the other Slone sister. I'm not the one you knocked-up." As the words tumbled off my tongue they felt foreign, not right.

"Rowan, stop!" He grabbed my arm.

"What?" I yanked away. "What do you want from me?" My tone dripped acid. How could I have been so stupid?

"Rowan, it's not what it seems."

"Bye, Mike." I ran up the stairs.

"It's not mine, Rowan!"

I didn't stop.

"She's lying!"

I was already through the large metal doors and running down the hall, his words trailing me like a disease. *It's not mine, Rowan. She's lying!*

I darted into chemistry class out of breath and panting. I slid into my seat just as Mr. Stewart was handing back our last test. He paused by my desk, lingering a moment too long, but I didn't look up.

I wiped my forehead with the back of my hand and took a deep breath. When I turned the test over, I saw a perfect score reflected at me in blaring red ink. I should've felt better, but I didn't.

I sat through social studies where the teacher lectured on goodness knows what. I didn't hear a word she said because the next class I had was biology. I did not want to see Mike. I knew, for sure, he could see it written all over my face: little mousy girl had a crush on him, poor thing. She must not have realized he preferred her voluptuous sister.

Damn him. Damn her.

When the bell rang, I snuck into the girls' bathroom and stayed there through the entire third period, taking deep, antiseptic-infused breaths. I had never skipped class. Never. Getting into college was too important. But today, well, today was today. And today didn't play by the rules, so I wouldn't either.

To keep my thoughts off things I didn't want to think about, I pulled out the novel we were going to start reading for English class: *Crime and Punishment* by Dostoyevsky. From page one, I was drawn to the dark tone and the psychological workings of Raskolnikov. It was a good way to spend fifty minutes, even if it was in the stall of the girls' bathroom with itchy fingers eager to slice, and an unsettled stomach ready to get rid of all that breakfast I'd eaten.

When the bell clanged, I shoved the book in my bag. The bathroom filled with girls glossing and teasing, or filing into stalls. I flushed the empty toilet and washed my hands at the sink, keeping my head low, not that anyone was paying attention.

Then I slipped into the throng of students, grateful for once that I was small enough to pass unseen. But then I heard his voice. Somewhere. Not near me but close enough.

I turned and slipped into the crowd going the other way. Without even bothering to go to my locker, I followed that crowd and took the long way to my next class.

Jess and I had English together, but she wasn't in there today. She'd texted something about having cramps and staying home. Her attendance record was as poor as my tardy record, but she didn't care. Her dad didn't seem like someone who cared either.

As promised, my English teacher introduced us to Fyodor Dostoyevsky. I sat in the back of the classroom with the novel open, urging my mind to reenter Raskolnikov's world and stay— for just a little while longer out of mine.

I DIDN'T see Mike the rest of the day. And when the final bell rang, I darted to my car, my insides ready to pour out of me after keeping it together for so long.

By the time I slammed my car door shut tears had already started and were streaming down my face like a waterfall. There were two thoughts getting equal billing in my head: Trina's evil-eyed glare as she pronounced Mike the father of her unborn child, and Mike's serious, stern stare as he said: *It's not mine, Rowan. It's not mine.*

I pulled out of the parking lot and sped down the road. I was going to work. And to Dan.

DAN SAT behind his desk in his closet-sized, personal office talking on the phone about wholesale versus retail value on a mid-sized pick-up truck that had been sitting on the lot for two months.

He was running his hairy hand over the thinning spot on his head. I wanted to tell him not to do that; that it may hurry along the balding process. But I had never really cared enough. Today, though, I may tell him.

When he saw me he didn't wave, smile, shoo me away. He stared at me unblinking as he listened to someone on the other end. Except behind his gaze was a look, an emotion, a *want* that made me gulp and have to clear my throat.

I turned away and started cleaning the mess that had accumulated since Mrs. Ames left this afternoon. He said *goodbye* to the person on the phone and I heard him get up from his chair. He walked into the outer office, a heavy sigh preceding him.

"Is everything okay?" I made my voice sound sweet.

He moved to my side. "Yeah. I can't seem to get rid of that truck. It's killing me."

I faced him and put my hand on my slender hip, pushing it out in a hopefully provocative way. "That's okay. I'm sure something will come up. You can always take it to an auction."

His eyes traveled over my body. "Yep. That's right. But I could use a better sale than what I'll get at the auction. Business hasn't been that good lately."

I twirled a strand of hair around my finger. "True. But it'll be okay. It's almost summer and everyone around here loves a pick-up truck in the summer. You'll sell it."

He scanned my face as if searching for a hint, an answer to an unasked question. Something was different; he just couldn't figure out what.

"So," I started, ready to give him a helping hand. "I've been thinking."

"Yeah?" He tilted his head. "About what?"

"About your proposition. You know. About going out. You got my text, right?"

He slid an inch closer. "Yeah. I got it." His voice fell deeper, huskier, though I'm not sure I'd ever heard anything *husky* before. But if husky had a sound his tone would've been it.

"Yeah. You know. Let's give it a try." I pulled out a tube of lip gloss that I'd stolen from Trina's makeup bag and swiped it across my lips.

I resisted the urge to lick my lips. Trina would've licked hers. And I had to force myself not to take a step back as he moved closer.

He put his hand over my hand which was back on my jutted-out hip, lip gloss discarded on the counter.

"That sounds great." His face was bending toward mine, his lips getting closer. I swallowed hard, but I didn't move back.

The door swung open. Our heads turned at the same time to find Jess glaring at Dan. He dropped his hand from my waist and darted into his office.

"What the *hell* was that?"

I waved a hand in the air. "It's nothing. Nothing." My shoulders fell forward and I felt this day would never, ever end.

"That sure looked like *something* to me, Ro. What's going on?"

"Nothing, Jess. Let it go." *I* wasn't even completely sure what was going on.

She yanked off her glasses and started cleaning them on the hem of her gray sweater, fast and furious. "Why is he touching you? Was he getting ready to *kiss* you?" She thrust her glasses back on her face.

He *was* getting ready to kiss me. Or at least it seemed that way. Is that really what I wanted?

Before I could linger on that question, Jess continued, "Rowan, he's an old man!"

"Not that much older than Paul," I spat.

My nerves felt frayed, raw. This was my best friend. And we were fighting over Dan. *Dan.* My creepy boss. But somehow that knowledge didn't make me back down from her glare. Or admit that I felt so lost right then that I would've done anything to feel better...wanted...alive.

Her jaw clenched. "Do not compare the two of them. That man is a creep!" Her voice was low but her words were lethal, full of knives.

I slammed my hands on the counter. "It's no different and you know it. There is no difference between Paul and Dan."

"Don't be a bitch, Ro."

I stormed into Dan's office, slamming the door behind me. Dan was back on the phone, and I leaned against the door, trying to calm my breath.

Jess and I had never argued. Never. But it had been such a bad day. Such a bad day.

The tears started deep in the back of my throat and worked their way upward, threatening to spill over and drown me in my own sorrow. I grabbed my backpack and just left.

I dug my nails into my arm, oblivious of the pain. It wasn't until I rubbed off the scab and blood soaked through my shirt that I stopped. I drove home, climbed through my window and wept into Scout's tiny back.

My phone dinged several text messages, but I didn't check a single one.

chapter nine

IF A zombie had infiltrated my body overnight, I would've felt more alive. Hollow, yet weighed down at the same time. Empty, yet full of so much *something*, I could barely sit up in bed.

It was another night spent with little sleep. Shutting off my mind was not an ability I had. Nor was shutting off my feelings. So I had studied. Again.

Tonight Mike and I would have to see each other to work on our report. Mr. Chambers was not known for being flexible and understanding so asking to switch partners was not an option. In fact, knowing his reputation for being the surliest teacher in the county, he'd move us into our own private room to complete the rest of the school year doing independent study. No one but the two of us. Not an option.

I forced my socked feet down the hall and into the shower. Today I had to talk to Jess. I couldn't lose the only friend I had.

Trina's door was closed and so was Mom's. I hadn't seen either one of them yesterday, which wasn't unusual, at least in Mom's case. I stopped by Trina's door but there was no sound. Maybe she was still asleep. Maybe the pregnancy was making her more tired than usual.

I flattened my palm against the cheap wood of her door then rested my forehead against it. My little sister. My used-to-be-so-sweet little sister. How had it come to this?

Then I thought about her and Mike *together*, and I shoved away from her door and stumbled into the bathroom.

I LOOKED for Jess in the parking lot but her bus sat along the curb, empty of the students. She hadn't waited for me.

My legs barely carried me into school. If I were a ghost, I wouldn't have felt more invisible as I walked down the hall. I couldn't feel anything anchoring me to this world, to my life. Would I just float away one day? Just disappear into the atmosphere? And would anyone even notice?

I was supposed to check-in with Miss J. Or was that yesterday? I didn't feel like talking to her so I got my books and meandered my way through the day like I'd been drugged, sliced open, then re-sewn with nothing but cotton filling my insides.

Finally, it was noon. I had skipped biology again and now the day was half over. If it wasn't the longest day of my life it was pretty darn close. Instead of taking my lunch break, I went to the library. I slid into a cubicle and let my head fall against the cold, smooth surface.

"I need to talk to you."

My head flew up to find Mike's face, with cheeks red and eyes bright, staring down at me. He pulled up a chair from the next desk and scooted so close our knees touched.

"You don't need to talk to me. You need to talk to Trina."

I scooted my own chair back, but he stopped it with his foot.

"Rowan, please."

I stared at him, trying to turn my former-cotton filling into steel. But it didn't work. Those green eyes, as dark as pine, were my undoing.

"Fine," I barked. "What is it? Why do you need to talk to *me?*"

"It's not mine."

"Then why would she say it is?" This shouldn't be so painful. Mike was nothing to me. It shouldn't matter if he had sex with my sister. And got her pregnant. It just shouldn't matter.

He shook his head, ran a hand through his hair. Dark circles lined his eyes and he looked pale, like he hadn't slept last night. Or the night before.

"I don't know. I mean. We have never...*done* anything!"

I stared at him. "You haven't...*done* anything? You didn't have sex with my sister and get her pregnant?"

"No!" he said.

Mrs. Grey *shushed* us from her desk across the room.

He leaned into my ear. I could smell his cologne and a faint trace of hair gel. "I have never had sex with your sister so I certainly didn't get her pregnant!"

"You're lying!" But my voice lacked the conviction.

He seemed to sense it too because he held my gaze, making me falter even more.

I leaned toward him. "Then who did?"

"I can tell you for sure it wasn't me. Look, I've wanted to ask you out all year; at least since I broke up with my ex-girlfriend. I wouldn't go and mess it up by having sex with your sister!"

My mouth dropped open. Was he lying? Was Trina? With sharp angles forming every word I spoke, I said, "Then why would she say you were the father? Answer me that." It wasn't difficult to make my words hateful. The mere thought of Mike and Trina together was enough to do that.

He put his hand under the desk and covered my knee. "I don't know. That baby is not mine. If she's even pregnant! Knowing your sister's reputation, it could be anyone's. But it's not *mine*."

I folded my arms over my chest and tried to will my leg not to shake. His hand was large, more than covering my skinny knee. And it was warm. Solid. Yet soft.

"I wouldn't mess around with your sister when you are the only Slone girl I'm interested in."

My breath refused to move.

"I've asked you two once to be quiet. This is study hall not social hour." The pinched face of Mrs. Grey peered at us over the rim of her bifocals. "If I have to tell you again, you will be given a detention slip."

Then the bell rang. I stood, my hands shaking so bad it took two tries to get a grip on my bag while Mike waited. He held the door open for me and we made our way into the hall. I kept my head down as Mike steered me through the crowd toward a corner, his hand swallowing my own.

"Look," he said. "Can we go somewhere and talk? I mean, leave?"

"Leave now?"

"I just have health. I can miss it. Coach is the teacher. What's yours?"

"Spanish. Trig."

"Please tell me you can miss it? Please, Rowan."

I leaned against the cool, tile wall. Mike hovered over me, one hand pressed against the wall by my head. Could I miss Spanish? I had an 'A' in the class. There were no absences on my record. If I had less than three absences in a class the entire year, I would be given an extra point on my final grade. And since I hadn't missed any, maybe I could miss just this one. The same was true with trig.

But more than that, the thought of spending one more moment in this school felt infinitely worse than being stuck in a dryer on the hottest setting. I needed air. And I wanted to hear what Mike had to say.

"Let's go." I wouldn't do this again.

It was a sunny day and warm for April. I pulled my hoodie off, careful not to let my long-sleeved shirt ride up my arm.

We moved toward our cars, parked near each other.

"Your ride or mine?" he asked.

"Mine. I have to be back in time for work." I shuddered at the thought.

"I have practice that I can't miss, but let's just get out of here for a little while."

Never had I heard a better idea.

We climbed into my car and I pulled out of the parking lot before I changed my mind.

"Where to?" I asked.

"Let's go to Beauty Mountain. We can sit and talk there. No one will bother us."

We were silent as I drove down Main Street. I clenched the steering wheel, willing my cheeks not to blush or my lips not to shake when I felt his eyes on me. He was watching me. Staring at my profile. I wanted to ask what he was thinking; why he was looking at me. But I didn't. Instead, I asked, "Did Trina tell you she blamed this on you?"

Out of my peripheral vision, I saw his head turn toward the road. The air in the car changed somehow, suddenly charged with tension, aggravation.

"No. That girl on the squad did. The one Trina is always hanging out with."

"Jennifer?"

"Yeah. Her. She called me last night, which was strange because I don't think we've ever exchanged two words. She called to tell me that Trina was pregnant and was going to tell people that I was the father."

"You're kidding? Jennifer did that?"

"Yep."

"Why would she go behind Trina's back?"

He shrugged. "I don't know. But that's how I found out. At first I didn't believe it. Then when I saw the look on your face yesterday, it was obvious that's the story she told."

I eased onto the single lane road that led to Beauty Mountain, winding up a steep incline. What he said made sense. If he was telling the truth.

Beauty Mountain was an isolated slat of flat land at the top of one of the surrounding mountains. Most kids went there to drink, make out; do all manner of things they preferred to keep quiet from the adults in their lives. It could be the spot where Trina had gotten herself pregnant, though when she'd had the time, I didn't know.

I parked on the side of the road. We got out, not speaking, and hiked the several yards to the natural overlook. Mike climbed onto a large rock then extended his hand. I grabbed it. With a swift and easy pull, I was up by his side. His calf, knee, hip and arm rested against my own and sent warmth shooting throughout my entire body.

The scenery helped clear my tumbling thoughts. The view was surreal. We were surrounded by sharp peaks encased in rich green. The mountains plunged into a deep ravine where a wide river flowed.

I took a deep breath, closing then opening my eyes. Mike was staring at me.

I chuckled, more from nerves than humor. "What?" I asked.

"Have you ever been here?"

I shook my head and turned to hide my blush. "No." Jess had mentioned something about coming here with Paul, but I'm not sure if she ever did. By my side, a black beetle scurried from the rock to the ground and disappeared from view.

"Rowan, do you believe me?"

I leaned over and tried to find the beetle.

"About your sister?"

I shrugged, noncommittal, not finding the beetle but not looking up either.

He scratched his finger against my shoulder. I rubbed the tickle away. He did it again. Finally I turned.

"Do you believe what I told you? That I'm not the father. Trina and I have never done anything."

Did I believe him? I wanted to believe him. And, actually I did, though the reasons why I believed Mike over my sister were too vague and deep-seeded for me to voice. When I asked myself would she do something like this just to hurt me? The only answer I had was she would.

"I believe you. I mean, I guess." I scooted an inch away. Sitting so close to him made it impossible to think. "Should I not?"

He closed that inch. "You should. And I'm really happy you do."

"Then tell me the whole story. Why would Trina say that you are the father?"

He breathed out his nose and bit his lip. "I don't know. It was weird. I was at practice yesterday. The cheerleaders were practicing at the end of the football field, like always. After practice was over, I came out of the locker room. No one else was around but Trina, who was leaning against the concession stand crying.

"I went over and asked her what was wrong." He laughed. "It was against my better judgment, but I couldn't just walk away from a crying girl."

I nodded. Oh, how I wished he had.

"She seemed really upset. It looked like she'd been crying for a while. She said that she was in big trouble." He chuckled through a deep frown. "Something told me to leave right then and there. That I didn't want involved in anything she was getting ready to say." He looked at me. "You and your sister are nothing alike."

"I know." I turned my profile to him. It was cooler here under the canopy of the trees and I pulled my hoodie back on. I thought about Trina. Did she end up going to school today? I hadn't seen her, but I often didn't. Ours was a large school, pulling in students from miles around. Most of her classes were in a separate wing altogether.

Was she sick this morning? Had Dad taken her to the abortion clinic on his own? Would I return to a sister no longer pregnant?

Mike continued, "She told me she was pregnant. I asked who the father was but she wouldn't tell me. She said your dad was going to kill her."

I nodded. Patches of clover and moss grew around the base of the rock. It looked so soft, I resisted the urge to move off the hard rock and nestle into it for a nap. "She never told you who the father was?"

"Eventually. She said it was Christian Dalton."

"Christian Dalton! The sophomore?"

He nodded.

"He's a black kid, right?" I was staring at him now.

"Yep."

I let out a whistle and slid off the rock. "Wow. That's why she said the baby's father was you?"

"I'm sure. She seemed really scared. She didn't tell me she was going to pin it on me. Jennifer told me later on. But, like I said, she seemed really scared and upset."

"As she should be. She's a knocked-up fifteen-year-old."

He nodded.

"Have you talked to her?"

"No."

"I wonder why she chose to pin it on you. I mean, it makes sense that she wouldn't want to admit that Christian was the father. My dad is not exactly racist, but he's also not very *accepting*. I guess that's the right word. But why you? There are several other guys she could've pinned it on. Like the guy I caught her making out with behind the concession stand the other day."

"I'm sure because she knew it would hurt you. That *me* being the father would hurt *you* the most."

My cheeks reddened and I laughed, unable to keep the twinge of hysteria out of it. I wanted to say, *that's ridiculous*. Or, *why would that bother me?* But she'd been right. Trina was very astute. She knew I liked Mike even though I never told her. Maybe she caught me watching him practice soccer. She was perceptive enough to know that it would hurt me and she'd said it anyway. She'd said it on purpose.

I hated her.

"Hey." He slid off the rock and stood before me. With a finger under my chin, he tilted my face up until I looked at him. At first

I wouldn't pull my gaze from the distant mountain top, but then I did. I looked at Mike, into his eyes, his soft expression, and I saw only good things there.

And then he kissed me.

His lips were soft, his breath minty. He was the third boy I'd ever kissed but the first one whose touch sent sparks straight from my mouth to my knees. I lifted to my toes and he wound his arms around my back, helping lift me higher.

His arms were as solid as a bar across my back, but so much warmer. He deepened the kiss, opening his lips. I responded by parting my own.

My thoughts evaporated. There was nothing left, nothing but a hazy contentment underneath the raging surge of blood pumping through me. I could kiss him forever.

So when he broke the kiss, I cursed my short stature. If I was taller, he wouldn't have broken it so easily. At least he didn't drop his arms.

"Rowan?" He looked over my face, stopping for several seconds on my lips.

"What?" My voice was hoarse.

Our noses were close; our lips nearly touching again. "I'm sure this will all blow over soon and it'll come out who the real father is."

"I hope so," I whispered. I couldn't think. The only thing that was clear was how close he was standing to me and that I wanted to return to that kiss more than anything I'd ever wanted in my entire life.

"And once the truth comes out, it'll be time to get ready for the Prom."

My stomach flipped.

"Will you go to the Prom with me?"

At first I was unable to answer the question. This was what I wanted: Mike Anderson asking me to Prom. Mike Anderson interested in *me*, not Trina, not anyone else.

But when I opened my mouth, what I found there wasn't an answer, but a question. "Why? Why me?"

"What do you mean?"

I shrugged, trying to find the right words, but coming up empty.

"There's just something about you, Rowan. You're *different* from other girls." His lips brushed mine. "Say you'll go to Prom with me." He kissed me again, leaving me with only one answer to that question.

I nodded, already tumbling into the sweet oblivion of Mike's kiss.

chapter ten

IT WAS nearly time for school to end when we left Beauty Mountain. As I drove, Mike's hand was on the back of my head, running his fingers through my hair. Twice I swerved off the road when I felt his eyes burning into me. He'd laugh, turn back toward the window, and keep rubbing my neck.

When I pulled into the school parking lot, he took his hand away, and my skin cooled from the loss of his warmth.

"Where are you going to go?" he asked after we got out of my car.

"I have to go to work. Then I guess I'll go home." Neither of those options was appealing. "Do you, um, still want to meet tonight? To work on the project?"

"Actually, I can't meet tonight. There's something at church my mom wants my dad and me to go to. Can you meet tomorrow? At seven?"

I nodded. It was Friday tomorrow. We were meeting on a Friday night.

Mike put his hands on my hips and brought his face close to mine. "I'll call you tonight?"

I nodded. Then I laughed, and even I was surprised by how genuine it sounded. "You can most certainly call me." Everything else slipped away like a whisper on the wind as he kissed me.

When he pulled away, his expression was changed. Before it was teasing and content. Now it was serious. "Rowan, you can call me any time, day or night. You know that, right? If things get crazy at home with Trina and your folks, or whatever, you can call me. My parents would understand and you could crash at my house. They're surprisingly cool. One of my sister's boyfriends stayed with us a while when he parents were in Europe."

He gave me a piece of paper with two phone numbers scrawled across it. His cell and his home. I nodded, swallowing the lump that formed in my throat. It was an odd thought, staying with Mike and his family. I almost laughed. But I didn't.

"Thanks," I said finally. "I'm sure it'll all be fine."

"Okay." He kissed me again. "Talk to ya later."

He jogged off toward the field.

I stood there longer than I needed then scanned the outside of the school, trying to find Jess. But she wasn't in the stream of people getting on the bus, so finally I pulled out my phone and sent her a text. I'd just gotten asked to the Prom by Mike Anderson. Someone needed to share this with me.

I'm sorry I texted.

I waited a few minutes to hear back from her, but my phone remained silent.

I have news I texted.

Still nothing.

Maybe she was at work. Mr. Sumners hated when she was late so sometimes she skipped last period to get there early, especially if he had a new shipment of books. But she usually answered her phone. At least when I called.

Finally, I drove to the car lot. I'd try her again in a little while.

TODAY WAS the beginning of the spring sale Dan always had in April, trying to move out old inventory and make room for new. So when I pulled in, there were streams of people, mostly men, in and out of the lot, looking at the trucks, negotiating price, discussing repairs.

Dan barely said two words to me. Which was fine. That meant we didn't have to talk about yesterday. When it was time for me to leave, Dan was with a customer. I didn't bother to wave goodbye as I got into my car and drove home.

THE HOUSE was dark as usual. The curtains were pulled tight on every window but mine, which stuck out like a naked, little hole. The front door was shut, a solid barrier between what was inside and what was outside.

Dad's truck wasn't there. It was getting dark and the temperature was dropping. I rubbed my right arm for warmth but left my other arm alone.

I let Levi off his leash to run around and then went into my room to see Scout. She was curled up on the floor by my bed. I scooped her up and held her close while I refilled her water bowl and poured food in her bowl.

I went back into the hall. Mom's door was shut, of course. And so was Trina's. The house looked exactly like it did when I'd left this morning, other than the antiseptic smell of cleaning supplies. Gran must've been here *again*.

The refrigerator was also full. Gran's only income was her social security check, but sometimes she went grocery shopping for me, since I was the only one in the house who kept the food stocked. I'd thank her next time I saw her, and offer to repay her, though I knew she wouldn't take the money. Maybe Dad would reimburse her.

Leaving the food untouched, I grabbed a glass of water and went back to my room, flopping onto the bed. Scout climbed onto my chest and licked my chin. I pulled a thread from my bedspread and jiggled it in her face. Her little paws tried to grab it but she couldn't. I laughed and didn't hear Trina open the door.

She stood in the open space, with tear-streaked cheeks and disheveled hair. Her T-shirt, the face of a cartoon cat imprinted on the front, was stained and too small. As were the tiny shorts she had on.

Rolling my eyes, I kept the thread dancing.

"You're not mad at me?" Her voice sounded young, with a little girl-like whine finishing each word.

"What did you say?"

"You're not mad at me?" She wrung the hem of her shirt between her hands.

"Why would I be? I know the truth." I forced light and air into my voice.

"What do you mean?" The little girl voice withered away.

I looked at her. "I know Mike's not the father. And I also know who is."

"Did you talk to Mike? Of course he would deny it." She blinked several times and then looked away. With clenched teeth, I went back to making the thread dance; something in me hardened to her words. I could almost feel the solid walls being built up around me.

"Rowan! Mike is the father. I've never had sex with anyone else."

"Um, okay," I said sarcastically.

She huffed. Tears started fresh down her cheeks. Her skin was blotchy and red. Her fists were clenched. I wouldn't have been surprised if she threw herself down on the floor, arms and legs kicking. But she did no such thing.

"Mike is the father. I should've known you wouldn't believe me. You're a terrible sister. I hate you. You ruin everything. And guess what, Ro. You. Always. Have."

I steeled myself. "Trina, it's not my fault you got pregnant. I didn't force you to have sex with Christian Dalton." It took great effort not to see the expression on her face. But I didn't look up. I didn't want her to see that I cared.

"Mike Anderson is the father." She slammed the door.

I blinked away the moisture behind my eyes and took a determined breath. I wouldn't let her mistake take Mike down.

Scout's string forgotten, I walked to my window and stared out into the night. We had neighbors, though you couldn't see their houses from my window. From this view, our home was as isolated and remote as if it was on a deserted island, or in an uninhabited forest.

How had our lives come to this? Trina pregnant at fifteen? Mom unable to get out of bed? Dad holding onto the resentment that his little boy was dead and I was the cause?

I tried to think about Mike, my good grade on the chem test, the fact that I only had one more year in this hell-hole of a house–about something positive. But I couldn't. My head hurt. Being in this house, surrounded by memories, guilt, and resentment–all those devastating things made it impossible to see the bright side of anything.

So I slid my hand between the mattresses and pulled out my razor. My arm looked like angry railroad tracks and I was adding more to it all the time.

I MUST'VE fallen asleep because I didn't hear a car pull up to the house, even though my window was open. But when the doorbell rang, I jolted upright, suddenly afraid of a repeat scene from the night before. I accidentally knocked Scout to the floor. She meowed in protest.

I looked out to the front yard. There was a police car parked there. Two uniformed officers, one male, one female, stood on our concrete porch. The doorbell rang again.

"Mom?" I walked out of my room.

There was no sign of Dad. They wouldn't be here about him, would they?

Please let everything be okay.

"Come here, Rowan." Mom stood at the opened door, waving the officers in. Trina sat huddled on the sofa, a blanket wrapped over her shoulders. She glanced up as I came down the hall but quickly looked away as I passed in front of her.

"What's going on, Mom?" I asked.

My mother's face was almost as red and blotchy as Trina's. Mom was dressed, at least, in black pants and a worn sweater. Her hair was combed and it looked like she'd taken a shower.

"Is it Dad?" I glanced from Mom to the officers. My stomach clutched into a knot.

"Rowan, sit down. This has nothing to do with your dad. These officers are here to ask Trina some questions." Her voice cracked.

I leaned against the counter, gripping its smooth surface. What had Trina done now?

"HE RAPED me," she said, in answer to the officer's question. "Mike Anderson raped me."

"What?" I stared between the officers and Trina. "Is that what she said?" I stomped to the middle of the room. "He didn't rape her! They didn't even have sex!"

All brows, except Trina's, rose in my direction.

"She slept with Christian Dalton." I pointed my finger at her. "And knowing her, did it willingly!"

Trina jumped off the couch. "Liar! You're just jealous because Mike wouldn't so much as look at you!"

Mom grabbed Trina to her chest. Trina buried her face so I couldn't see her lying eyes.

"You little bitch," I spat. "You're just afraid to admit who the real father is!"

"Miss, what is your name?" interrupted the female officer. She pulled out a notebook and readied her pen. She stepped closer to me.

"Rowan Slone. That liar's older sister."

"Rowan, please! Your sister is very upset!" Mom stroked Trina's hair. I couldn't see my sister's face but the thought of the smirk that likely rested there made my vision turn red.

"Mom, she's lying! She got knocked-up by Christian Dalton!"

"Miss." The female officer stepped toward me. "Who is Christian Dalton?"

I glared at Trina's bent head. "A kid at school. Sophomore. And he's black which is why she's lying."

Mom paled. The officers stared between the three of us. The male officer had his hand on his gun holster. I didn't know if that was an automatic reaction to tense situations or if he thought we were really out of control. Probably the latter and he was very much correct. Our family *was* out of control.

"Trina?" Mom whispered into my sister's bowed head. "That's not true. Is it, Trina?"

Trina stayed quiet while I glared at her blonde head. What an interesting call this was going to turn out to be for the officers.

Finally, she looked up. Her expression was sad, so devastatingly sad, that I just knew she was going to tell the truth. She looked at me as tears streamed down her face, pleading at me with her clear blue eyes. My little sister, whose golden locks I used to braid into pigtails. My sister who used to think of me as her very own teddy bear and would pull me tight within her arms when she was sleeping.

I would forgive her. After all of this, I would forgive her.

But then she said, "Mike Anderson held me down behind the concession stand at the field and raped me. He forced me to have sex with him and now I've not only been raped, I'm pregnant. With his child."

"*No!*" I lunged for her. The female officer caught me in her iron arms. I thrashed. I kicked. I clawed at her arms. "No! You're a liar! Mike would never touch you!" I was screaming. Trina was crying. Mom was white, like she was about to slip into a coma.

Then Dad walked in the house.

"What's going on here?" he demanded. "Why are the police in my house?" He looked at Mom. "What did you do? Or was it them?" And he flicked his head with the word *them*, like we were the neighbor's dogs barking outside.

"Sir," said the male officer. "Please have a seat and we can figure out exactly what is going on."

"You're damned right I'll have a seat. It's my own house, for Christ's sake." He fell into the chair then glared at us all.

"Sir, what is your name?"

"Jack Slone. What's yours?"

"Sir, my name is Officer Calhoun and this is my partner, Officer James."

"What are you doing here?"

"Mr. Slone, your daughter has made a complaint against a fellow student, a Mr. Mike Anderson."

"What's her complaint?"

"Rape."

His lips pulled into a thin line and he stared at Trina. She didn't return his gaze, though. She had re-buried her head in Mom's chest. I hated her at that moment with a ferocity that turned my limbs rigid.

Dad pulled his eyes from my sister to my mom. She wouldn't look at him either. Instead, she laid her head on top of Trina's, like she was smelling her shampoo. Then he looked at me. I was held in a bear-hug by the female officer but when I released my grip on her arms, she lessened her grip on my body. Then she pulled away altogether, like she could sense there was no fight left in me. But she was wrong about that. I wouldn't let Trina pin this on Mike.

"Rape? Mike Anderson?" His voice was hard, steady. His fingers wrapped over the armrests, the tips white from the force of his clench. "Is *that* how you got pregnant?"

Trina nodded but did not lift her head.

"That Anderson boy raped you and got you pregnant?" he repeated. Each word was like a ten-ton boulder falling onto the ground, shaking the floor beneath us all. "Dr. Anderson's boy?"

Somehow Trina's size shrank, like someone released all the air in her body. She melted into Mom, clutching the sides of her arms. I could hear her shaking breaths each time she inhaled and exhaled.

"Trina, look at me. Now." His words were lethal, full of sharp edges, even though he didn't raise his voice. "Is this true?"

Trina's head lifted. Her eyes were a watery, crystal blue; shiny and swimming. Her lips shook and she pulled her bottom lip between her teeth, biting down hard enough to break the skin.

"Yes. It's true."

AN HOUR later, the officers left. I don't know how the rest of their time here went down because after Trina's last declaration, I went after her again. I almost had a handful of her blonde hair within my fist, but the strands fell through my fingers as the officer yanked me away with so much force, I got whiplash.

This time I was forced into my room and told not to come back out. Before I shut my door, I saw Officer James place her tall body at the end of the hallway, blocking me from my lying sister.

That was smart because at that moment I could've killed her. I didn't recognize her as my little sister. She was no one I knew. And no one I ever wanted to know.

chapter eleven

ANGER SIMMERED in my blood like a pot about to boil over. I wasn't sad. Depressed. I was full of rage and couldn't calm my shaking fingers. After the police left, the house settled into a black chasm of quiet. No one yelled. No one cried that I could hear. It was as silent as death.

Dad was probably still sitting in his chair, wondering what had happened to us all. Mom would have hurried right to bed, quickly comatose and unresponsive. Who cared where Trina was?

Unable to stand being there any longer, I got up before dawn. After a few minutes in the bathroom, I changed my clothes. Then I slipped out of the house, going out my window. I wanted to see Mike. Before I started my car, I sent a text:

> Meet me at the gas station. The one open all night. We need to talk.

He had a right to know what awful accusations were coming his way. I prayed he was up, though I had no reason to think he would be. But still, I took off down the road not caring who I woke up with the roar of my engine.

The gas station was just a mile away. There were several stations along the interstate, one even in town; but I wanted to go to the one that I knew would be open at five in the morning, and that also had a mart where I could get coffee. Just as I put the car in *park* in front of the store, my phone dinged.

Be there in ten the message read.

Air seeped out of my chest and I hadn't realized I'd been holding it. Did he know what Trina was doing? After he found out, would he still talk to me? Would he still want to go to Prom? Somehow I doubted it. And I couldn't blame him.

With sleeves pulled over my hands, I went into the store, passing by the clerk without a glance. The coffee station had four steaming pots ready for all the early morning customers. I picked up one and poured two coffees. After four packets of sugar in each cup, and five creamers, I figured they would taste good enough. Then I grabbed a couple of doughnuts and went to the counter to pay, never once looking at the man behind the counter, even though I could feel him watching me. Guess there weren't many girls my age in here at this hour.

As I pushed through the door, a truck from the power company pulled in and two middle-aged men got out. I recognized one as a friend of Dad's, but I slipped into my car before he saw me. Then I waited, not touching the coffee or the doughnuts.

Several minutes later, a car pulled in beside mine. Mike slid into the passenger seat and slammed the door. He kept his face forward, his jaw clenched. The store's light showed deep shadows under his eyes.

"Would you like a drink?" I held out one of the coffees. "I put in a ton of milk and sugar. I can't believe people drink this stuff without it." I forced a chuckle. "It tastes awful otherwise." My voice trailed off as I watched him. He was quiet. Too quiet. "So you know?"

"Yep. I know. Police were at my house last night. It seems I'm under suspicion for raping your sister."

His words fell flat and toneless. The two men from the power company walked out of the store. Another car pulled in. Then another. Soon the lot was full. The world lay in a gray haze all around us, full of shadows and clouds. I shivered.

"I'm so sorry," I said, finally.

He grunted. "Yeah. Me too."

He wouldn't look at me and his tone was distant, curt. I rubbed my left arm until his silence wasn't so painful.

"Can I do anything to help? I told the officers that she was lying." I watched him from the corner of my eye and drew my knees up under my chin.

A young woman dressed in a pink nurse's uniform entered the store. She went straight to the coffee station and pulled out the largest Styrofoam cup they sold.

"I think they know she's lying," he said. "Or at least suspect it."

"What can I do?" I leaned toward him. I put my hand on his arm and he stared down at it, as if he wasn't sure what it was.

"Get her to tell the truth. I'm going to lose everything if this keeps on. Even if it's not proven. The accusation is enough. I'll lose any chance at a scholarship." He snorted. "My dignity. I'll lose everything."

"I'll try, Mike. I promise. I don't think Dad believes her either." My words were shaped by the need to have him know that I was on his side. It bothered me only a little that I was choosing a boy's word over my own sister's. And there was only a very fleeting moment that wondered, what if she was telling the truth?

Unfortunately, I knew Trina. She'd said that Mike was the only guy she'd had sex with. But when she was fourteen, I found her and a guy in her bedroom after school one day. And it was obvious they weren't playing cards. My little sister was a liar. Was she just being the girl who cried wolf, or was there truth to her words?

WITH MY head a jumbled mess, unable to trap and consider any one thought, I stayed quiet. We sat there until the gray sky was replaced with long strokes of reds and pinks.

Finally, when the clock turned to seven, I said, "I think we need to go. I can't miss school. Or be late." I also wanted to break the silence. It had grown heavier than an avalanche falling over our heads.

"I'll meet you there." He slid out of my car. He never once looked at me and I sat on my hand to keep from reaching out to him. The coffees remained untouched; the doughnuts uneaten, their sugary smell filling the car with sickening sweetness. I hopped out and threw them away before getting back in my car and following Mike to school.

We were early and the lot was only half full. I parked beside his car, but when I got out, he didn't. I walked to his window.

He ran a hand through his hair and looked years older than eighteen. "I can't go in there. Not today."

I nodded.

"Not with this accusation hanging over me. I'm sure she's told everyone at school. Word travels fast in a small town."

There was a circle of pain around my heart at seeing him that way, knowing that my own sister had caused this. And she'd done it to spite me. I hated her. I hated my sister. Not only was she a liar, but she was going to cost me Mike, one of the few bright spots in my life.

"I'll talk to her today." My voice sounded pleading to me. How did it sound to him?

"Okay." His tone so expressionless, it sounded like a robot's. He put the car in *drive*. "I'm going to go."

I studied his face, willing him to say something else, feeling him slip away from me. "Mike," I pleaded.

Finally, he glanced up. "It's okay, Rowan. I don't blame you."

But something about the way he pulled his eyes from my face, quickly, like it hurt to look at me, told me that his statement wasn't entirely true. I may not have caused this mess directly but the accuser was my sister. Guilty by association.

Without another glance, he pulled out of the parking lot and drove away.

I MADE it to my first class just as the bell was ringing. Then I went to my next class, and my next, keeping my head down and trying to ignore the stares of everyone I passed. Halfway through the day, I went to my locker and fell against it. The metal was cool against my back, solid, and supportive. With my eyes closed, I focused on the sounds of the hallway–the screech of sneakers, the giggles of girls, the low-pitched drone of junior and senior boys talking to one another.

"Ro, what the hell is going on?"

My eyes flew open to see Jess standing in front of me, hand on her hip. Today her cherry-red hair was pulled away from her face with a black headband. She had colored the tips purple. Black eye liner made her large blue eyes pop behind the glasses. She towered over me and when I lifted my head to look at her, I was moved by the concern I saw and I tried to smile. Tried to show her how glad I was she was talking to me.

But I couldn't. My head fell back against the locker with a bang.

All I could do was shrug my shoulders because words wouldn't come to me. Tears filled my eyes and I bit my lip. I hated to cry.

But when Jess reached out and rubbed my arm, and I looked back at her, I lost it. Tears flooded from my eyes like a burst dam and my shoulders shivered under the weight of my life.

Jess wrapped her arms around me, pulling me close to her body. "Shhh," she whispered into my hair.

But I couldn't stop. I welcomed the shield of her body, happy that my own stature could be so easily hidden. And I wept.

Jess forced a laugh. "People are staring, Ro. This is how rumors get started. Two girls making out in the hall…"

I tried to laugh, managed a hiccup, and then lifted my head.

"So, the rumors are true?" Jess pushed up her glasses.

I glanced up. "Which ones?"

"Trina's pregnant?"

I nodded, eyes welling with fresh tears.

"Who's the father?"

So *that* rumor hadn't started. But I couldn't bring myself to say it, to admit that my sister had cried foul and blamed my Prom date for not only knocking her up but for raping her.

I shook my head, unable to voice any words. In my pocket sat a cool, thin razor. I hadn't needed its release last night when anger made me see nothing but flames and heat. But now it was calling to me and my fingers itched to touch it. I needed to get to the bathroom. My fingers shook with anticipation.

"I can't get into it now. Let's catch up later, okay?" I took a step away from her. "Too much to even get into now. Oh, by the way, Mike asked me to Prom." My voice sounded dead to me, shaped by none of the excitement that should come with that statement.

"Ro, that's great!" But I could tell by the somber expression on her face that she barely registered what I said.

"Yeah, that's great."

"Something else is wrong, though." Jess knew me very well.

I pulled in a deep breath. "Yeah. Trina is saying that the baby is Mike's." Jess' mouth fell open. "But, it's really Christian Dalton's. The sophomore. Oh, but in order to keep from getting killed by Dad for getting knocked-up by a black kid, she's now saying that Mike raped her." Once I started, the words poured out in a flood.

"What? Are you *kidding* me?" She yanked off her glasses and stared at me.

I shrugged, reaching into my pocket to touch the razor. The tardy bell rang and I pulled my hand out to grab books from my locker.

"I gotta go. I can't be late."

"Let's meet after school. We can talk more. Do you have to work?"

"I don't know. I just don't know. I'll send you a text." I didn't want to think about work, Dan, Trina, home.

"Hey." She put her hand on my arm. "I'm sorry about the other day."

I swallowed against the lump in my throat. "Me too."

I pulled her into a quick hug, then darted into the girls' bathroom where I locked myself in a stall and pulled the razor out of my pocket.

THE REST of the day passed in a fog. Finally, the bell rang and I darted outside, gulping air like I'd been suffocated. And I had to go to work and deal with Dan.

When I got there, he was outside with a customer. He glanced up when I got out of the car. I went into the office and started going through the day's paperwork.

The sale was still going on and the paperwork was a mess. I organized the receipts in one pile, invoices in another and in a final pile, all parts order forms. After I wiped fingerprints and coffee rings off the counter, I refilled the cups in the holder beside the water dispenser. I put a fresh roll of paper towels in the bathroom, and then gave a quick spray of air freshener.

Dan shook hands with the customer, and then started toward the office, leaving the man roaming among the vehicles, kicking tires and peering in windows. The man got into one of those ancient, impossibly long cars and sputtered out of the parking lot.

"Hi." Dan stopped in the doorway.

"Hey."

His eyes burned into me. "Is something wrong?"

"I guess not."

"Rowan, what's going on? Is it about your friend and what happened the other day?"

I guess he meant Jess. He probably thought his chances of us dating were greatly reduced if my best friend didn't like him.

I grabbed a broom and started sweeping.

"There's too much going on to get into and it has nothing to do with Jess." I wove the broom around the chairs. "Is that guy going to come back? Looks like he needs a new car." I flipped my head toward the window even though the man was long gone.

"He'll be back tomorrow with cash." He didn't move from the doorway and I had to walk right past him to sweep the other side of the room.

"I don't know what to say." I sighed. "My sister is pregnant. She says it's one guy's. I hear it's not that guy's but actually a different guy's. I confronted her about that and then she turned around and said she'd been raped by the first guy she named."

"Raped? Rowan, was your sister raped?" He walked toward the counter and leaned against it, arms folded over his chest.

I put the broom away. "That's what she said. The police were over last night to talk about it."

"But you don't think she was? That she was raped?"

I shook my head, wishing I had something else to clean. "I don't think she's telling the truth. It would be like Trina to get knocked-up then blame it on someone else. Someone more acceptable."

"I see. But would Trina really go that far? Blame someone for rape who hadn't even touched her?" I turned my back to him and started to line up the four black chairs that sat in the waiting room. "Isn't that a bit extreme? I mean, I don't know your sister, but really."

I slammed the chairs into line then scooted them across the floor so they were even. "I don't know. Trina is capable of many things normal people wouldn't do."

He was quiet for several moments. I knew he watched me as I fiddled with the plastic blinds, trying to create a perfect horizontal line across the bottom. "Okay," he said finally. "Is there anything I can do?"

"Nope."

"Rowan?"

"What?" I demanded.

"Do you really think Trina would make this up? I mean, isn't it possible that this guy she's accusing actually *did* rape her?"

I kicked a chair across the floor. "I gotta go." I darted for my backpack. "That okay with you?"

He hesitated. I'd been bailing out on work a lot this week. "Sure, Rowan. You have a lot going on."

"Hmpf."

"Rowan?"

"Hmm?" I focused on finding my keys.

"Rowan?"

I looked up. My keys dangled from my forefinger.

"Are you okay?" There was something in Dan's expression that aggravated me. He cared too much, maybe. I don't know what it was; only that it made my skin crawl when I met his gaze.

"I'm fine. Just like always." I pushed through the door.

I HAD to check on Scout and Levi. No one else fed or gave Levi water and now with Scout, there was no way I could stay away that long. I drove home and pulled into the driveway, easing past Dad's truck and parking beside the house.

Light filtered through the heavy curtained windows, but the house still looked closed-off, resistant somehow. I didn't hear shouting but that didn't mean the mood inside was a good one. Levi greeted me and I bent to my knees to pet him.

The world lay quiet around us, deceptively peaceful and serene. Chills spread across my skin, even though it was warm out. The back of my neck prickled and my muscles were tense and uncomfortable. I was stretching just as a car pulled into the driveway.

It wasn't a car I recognized; an old sedan that looked straight out of a seventies cop movie. But I did recognize the driver. It was Christian Dalton.

Levi whimpered and I loosened my grip around his neck, not even realizing how tightly I was holding onto him. Christian didn't see me in the shadows, but I watched him shut the car door and walk toward our house. His hands were shoved low in his jeans' pockets. His hair was closely cropped, perfect for showing off his angular face.

My phone dinged a new text message, but I didn't bother to check it. Lights were on in my parents' room, which sat closest to the side of the house where I huddled with Levi. Trina's room was just down the hall from there, and her lights were also on. Further down the hall was my room, the only bedroom window at the front of the house. That window was black.

Christian rang the doorbell. No one answered the door for several moments but then Dad's voice said, "Can I help you?"

I could only see the porch from the side and Dad didn't come out of the door. What was the expression on his face? Anger? Feigned curiosity? Barely veiled impatience?

He would be civil, polite to Christian. That is, until he found out he was the father of Trina's baby. There would be no civility then.

"Sir," I heard Christian say. "My name is Christian Dalton. Can I speak to Trina?"

"Why do you want to speak to my daughter?" Dad's voice was deep, gruff.

"Sir, Trina is a friend of mine. I'd just like to talk to her a moment."

"Trina!" Dad boomed. "There's a boy named Christian here to see you!"

I could see it now. Trina would slowly make her way toward the door, eyes downcast. She wouldn't want to come, but even she wouldn't push back at Dad. And Dad, he would stay by the door, arms crossed, looking every bit the fearsome prison guard. If Christian was smart, he would turn around and leave.

chapter twelve

BUT HE didn't. "Trina, can I talk to you outside?" Christian asked into the house.

"You can speak to her right here." Dad's voice was full of concrete walls and razor wire.

There was a pause, one of those *and time stood still* moments. Trina was still huddled inside the house and I could only see Dad's shadow. Christian, who was almost as tall as Dad, dropped his hands to his sides. His shoulders fell forward.

"Trina," Christian said. "Leave Mike out of this. He doesn't deserve to be dragged into this."

"Mike?" Dad asked. "Mike, the boy you say raped you?"

"Sir," started Christian, but he didn't finish his sentence.

I could see part of Dad's body now, straddling the doorway. He was looking inside the house. Christian didn't move away and I really wished he would.

"Trina, answer the question."

Trina's cries wafted out into the night. I stepped around the corner.

"Why is this boy here?"

No answer.

"Why is this boy here?" Dad thundered and I jumped. Trina's crying grew louder. "Why is he here?" Waves of icy chills spread over my skin. Christian eased down the steps until he stood on the grass.

"I'm here, sir," he said, "to ask your daughter to tell the truth."

"Yeah? And what truth is that?"

Christian straightened his spine, as if pulling to his full height brought with it the courage of Achilles. He was almost as tall as Dad, but missed the mark in weight by at least thirty pounds.

"The truth is that Mike did not rape her. And the father of her baby is *me*. And not by rape. I promise you, it was consensual."

Trina whimpered somewhere just inside the door.

"What did you say?" my dad seethed. Though I couldn't see his face clearly, I could picture it in my mind's eyes. His teeth were clenched; his lips pulled back like a feral lion.

Christian cleared his throat. "Sir, I am the father of your daughter's baby. Not Mike Anderson." He projected his voice; like the louder he spoke, the more credible he sounded.

"Get off my property!" Dad shouted.

Christian didn't move.

"I said to get off my property before I grab my shotgun. There is no law against me defending my property!"

Christian backed toward his car. He didn't run, which I would've done. He didn't even walk fast. He opened his car door, but just before he slid inside, yelled, "Trina, tell the truth!"

"Get off my property!" Dad roared.

Christian got into his car and peeled out of the driveway. It was dark now, everything cast in black; everything that the lights from the house didn't reach. Even the moon was hiding. I wished I could've been up there with it.

"What was that boy saying, Trina?" The screen door slammed shut behind him. "Did you screw that kid? Is he your baby's father?" Dad's voice was full of fire and volcanos and hurricanes and tsunamis. "Trina!" he yelled again. "Is he the father?"

Trina's sobs carried through the screen door and rolled out into the yard. Then she screamed and something hit the floor. My eyes shut against the sound but nothing could keep the echo away.

"Amy! Your daughter got knocked up by some black kid! Did you know that, Amy? Can't you do any better by your daughters than to raise a slut? A no-good whore who will screw anything she sees?"

Something crashed. It sounded like a table falling over, a lamp smashing into the floor.

"Jack, please." Mom's voice pierced the night air.

"Don't *Jack, please* me! The apple didn't fall far from the tree, did it?" His tone was full of hate and disdain. "Whoring around in high school, getting knocked-up. Do you think she was trying to trap that Anderson boy like you trapped me?"

Something else crashed. "Trina! Do you think the Andersons wouldn't notice that baby looked nothing like their son?"

My ears vibrated with his fury. I stepped toward the porch, ignoring the voice inside my head that told me to run.

Get away from there.

Go to Dan's.

Go to Gran's.

Go to Mike's.

But I couldn't do any of those things. My feet would only take me toward the light, the door, the catastrophe unfolding behind it. At the bottom step, I stopped.

"You're nothing but a no good whore. Just like your mother."

"Daddy, please!" Trina cried. I heard what sounded like a smack. Trina screamed again.

Where was my mom?

"I'm leaving and I want you out of this house before I get back!" He tore through the door and was on the porch before I could move out of sight.

"Daddy!" Trina stumbled out behind him.

He faced the door, his hands clenched by his sides. "I never want to see you or your bastard baby ever again."

He stormed to his truck and slammed on the gas. The truck skidded out of the driveway.

"Daddy!" Trina screamed.

But he was gone. I took one step, then another, easing toward her. I felt like I was in a trance. Like what had just happened was in a different time mode. If a switch was flipped and time returned to normal, would it wipe out everything that had just happened?

Trina was leaning against the wall, her hands on her stomach. She hiccupped between sobs. I could see Mom's shadow fall across the porch. She was at the door but she was not coming outside. She was not going to console her daughter.

Trina looked shrunken, helpless…lost. Her shoulders had grown thin and bony. Was it the baby? Too much cheerleading practice? She was starting to look more like me.

"Trina?" I stayed on the bottom step.

Her eyes were glassy and red. They hardened in their focus on me. "Did you tell Christian to do this?"

"Tell him to do what?" I stopped mid-step at the fire in her words.

She pushed off the wall and turned toward me. "Tell Christian to come here and say that he's the baby's father?" It sounded like she was struggling to speak; like it took extreme effort to form words and release them from her lips.

"What? Trina, what are you talking about? Of course not."

"You couldn't stand it, could you? Couldn't just let this family live in peace for one single minute."

I felt like we were on two different trajectories, speaking the same language but with vastly different meaning.

"Trina, I'm not the one who came home pregnant." My words were soft.

The sound she made was a cross between a guffaw and a hiccup. Maybe a snort. It was an ugly sound and I cringed.

"What's wrong with you?" I reached out a hand to her, not really wanting to touch her, but not able to keep my hands by my side. She moved out of my reach.

"There's nothing wrong with me that can't be traced back to you. There's nothing wrong with this family that can't be blamed on *you*."

The air in my lungs evaporated like someone had hooked a vacuum up to my chest and flipped the switch *on*. I put my hands up. *Don't go there. Please don't go there.*

"You're the one to blame for everything wrong with this family!" Her voice rose with each spoken word and her eyes darkened with unspoken meaning. "Dad would be happy." She waved her hands through the air, slicing her palms with each word she spoke. "Mom wouldn't be in bed all the time like a depressed whale!" Her tone was raspy, raw.

"Trina, please stop." I tried to pull oxygen into my lungs.

"It changed everything, didn't it?" She released her words in short spats. I could almost see them; like when they left her lips, they took on a physical form. Little balls of crusty blackness, their insides full of hidden, yet raging lava. And that lava shot out of the blackness as she spewed the words at me.

How could she blame me for Aidan's death? How could Dad? Mom? How could I still blame myself?

Once Aidan died, the blame had washed over me wave after wave. It was a look, an attitude, a mood that grew like a weed in our family. But it was rarely spoken about, said out loud.

"Mom wouldn't come out of her room," I whispered. My hands and my knees shook like I was standing on a dryer.

No one ever said, *Rowen, you killed your brother*. Or, *It's your fault that he died*. But the blame was there. It was as constant and as real as the trees that grew outside of our home. I was blamed for the demise of our family. And I had only been ten.

A feeling almost unfamiliar to me started deep in my gut. It started with a bubble, like water on the brink of a boil. Then it got stronger, hotter, and wouldn't be contained. It was anger. Anger at my mother for being all but dead and not protecting us. Anger at my father for being a bully, enveloped in his sorrow and his rage. Anger at my sister, standing in front of me, her stomach still as flat and taut as the other fifteen-year-old girls at school. Anger at her for getting knocked-up and for now blaming me.

"I'm not the one who got pregnant, Trina." My tone was full of the rage simmering in my blood. "I didn't make the stupid decision to let myself get knocked-up. You can't blame me for that."

It felt good. The anger fueled me somehow, and it gave me energy. I balled my fists and leaned my chest forward.

I took another step. "So, you take yourself and your little baby and leave. Just like Dad said!"

She stumbled backward as my words got louder and louder.

"I'm going to make something of myself. I'm going to graduate high school. You're going to be stuck at a girls' home for young mothers. Then I'm going to go to college while you're stuck bottle feeding a baby. Then," I was shouting now, "I'm going to go to veterinary school. I'm going to become a veterinarian and I'm going to leave this shit town! And guess what, Trina. I'm *never* coming back!"

I pushed past Mom who was standing just inside the house. I didn't even acknowledge her or the tears that streamed down her face. I scooped up Scout in my room, and ran back out of the house. I left Mom crying in the family room, likely already on her way to the bed where she would spend the next several days. I left Trina crying on the porch. I left the guilt and blame that had hovered over me since I was ten years old.

Screw this family.

I couldn't wait for graduation to get out of here. I couldn't wait for Mike.

And I saw my future clearly for the first time ever. Dan was the answer. Dan was the only one who could get me out of my life. Once I turned eighteen, there was nothing anyone could say.

chapter thirteen

I LOADED Levi and Scout into the car. I had just shut the passenger side door when headlights illuminated the driveway. Squeezing my eyes shut, I tried not to look up. There would be no one coming to the house that I wanted to see.

The engine died. The car door opened. It slammed shut.

"Amy!" Dad bellowed.

I squeezed my eyes even tighter.

"Amy! Get out here!"

His words were full of rage. Any anger I'd tasted earlier was gone, squashed in the overwhelming fury of his.

Trina, whimpering, eased off the porch and slid down the side of the house. Her eyes were large, watery, the terror not veiled at all. I stood frozen by my car, watching him stomp toward the house. He stumbled over his own boots but righted himself.

"Amy!"

Then he saw me. He stopped on the bottom stair, turning first his head toward me, then, as if remembering there was more, his body. Trina stopped too, pressing herself flush against the house. If I didn't know she was there, I wouldn't have been able to see her in the darkness.

I gripped the car door, trying to steady my wobbling knees. Dad's eyes were black, dark; focused like a wolf.

"Come here," he commanded.

I couldn't move. Trina whimpered but he didn't seem to hear.

"Now!"

I let my fingers slide off the cool metal. One footstep. Then another. He had me locked in the forward motion, even though I knew that moving toward him was the last thing I should do. But I couldn't help it. In his stare was my sentence. In his command was my action. I was powerless.

He didn't move to meet me. My feet were like lead but mobile, moving me toward those eyes. The light of the porch lit his face, making his skin look pale, sallow. There were pink etches across the apples of his cheeks.

Then I couldn't help it. My feet stopped. I was almost to the bottom step but couldn't continue forward.

"Rowan," he said, his voice lethal.

My knees buckled but I pressed a hand against the house. I steadied myself just enough to remain upright.

"Rowan."

It was a command even my shivering legs couldn't ignore. So I stepped forward. I felt the palm of his hand against my cheek before I realized he had even moved. I stumbled back, but I didn't fall.

Two steps and he was before me. My hand covered my cheek. He whipped his hand in an arc across his chest, then hit me with the back of his hand. I slammed into the dirt. I landed hard. My dad was a strong man. Trina's cries grew louder, or maybe it was the ringing in my ears.

"Get up."

No. If I got up, he'd hit me again. No. I wouldn't get up.

"Jack! Stop!"

Mom ran out of the house and grabbed his arm. Dad shoved her off. I didn't look up at him but I felt his eyes burning their rage into me.

"Jack!" she said again. "Don't do this."

"Don't do what, Amy? Discipline my own daughter? After this one," he waved his hand at me, "I'll teach that other girl what happens when she gets pregnant."

Trina wailed and disappeared completely. Dad heard her, though. "Stop right there, Trina. I'm going to teach both of you girls a lesson you'll never forget. So the two of you don't turn out like your good-for-nothing mother here."

I scampered back. "What did I do?" I shrieked. The sting across my cheeks emboldened me. "I'm not the one who is pregnant!" I struggled to make my eyes focus.

He lunged forward, slamming his fist into my face. Black colored my vision. Like looking through a shadow, I could just make out his outline, standing over me. Stabbing pain throbbed in my head.

"*You* are responsible for the death of my son!"

He looked around; his glare resting on Mom then Trina.

"Trina, come here."

She didn't respond.

"Trina!"

She stumbled into the light. Her face was pale, though she didn't look frightened. She looked numb; like she didn't think or feel a thing.

"Come here," he demanded.

Her head moved up and down. She took another step. Her shoulder leaned against the outside of the house as she moved up the porch stairs, past my mom who reached out a hand as if to brush the hair off her shoulder. Her caress fell short, though, never actually touching Trina as she passed and moved down the other side's steps.

Then Trina's feet gave way under her and she fell. She was only a few feet from me. I pushed up onto my hands and knees.

"If you touch her, I'll kill you," I said.

Dad's head whipped around. I struggled to my feet, willing my spinning head to stop. I didn't fall, though. I clenched my fists, planted my feet. I tried to focus on his crotch from my blurry vision. All I needed was one kick. One good kick.

Then sirens pierced the quiet. Two police cars lurched into the driveway, slamming into a stop in front of our house. Red lights flashed across us all. A neighbor must've heard the shouting and called the police. Or maybe Christian had a premonition as he peeled out of our driveway that this issue was far from over.

Dad moved forward, on now-steady feet, to meet the officers as if he didn't have a care in the world. Four of them jumped out of the two cars and ran toward us, shouting. I bent to touch Trina's shoulder and she looked up at me. Her blue eyes were glassy and her skin was white. She looked like a china doll.

I fell to my knees and pulled her to me. My face throbbed and the vision in one of my eyes was slightly distorted, but I clutched her to me, ready to protect her from whatever came next.

The world swirled around us. I think an officer spoke to me, though I don't know what he said. Dad's voice droned on nearby but the words he spoke were muffled behind the ringing in my ears. At some point I heard my mom's voice. Then I was vaguely aware when the officers cuffed my dad and led him away. Someone said something about an ambulance.

But I just sat there, Trina whimpering in my lap as I stroked her hair.

MINUTES, OR hours later, Gran showed up. She eased Trina from my lap and half-carried, half-pulled her inside the house. I didn't realize Levi was even beside me until his head replaced Trina's in my lap. Gran must've let him off his leash. I curled over his solid body and his welcomed warmth.

Gran returned. "Rowan?" She sat beside me. "Look at me."

I turned my head.

She gasped. "Oh, my sweet baby." She pulled me to her and kissed my head. "Oh, my sweet baby." Under her breath, she said, "Damn that man. Damn that man."

I ignored her. I'm sure she wanted to kill him. Maybe she really would.

"I'm going to take you to the hospital."

"I don't need to go to the hospital." My voice was full of cotton and lead.

"Honey, let's just go in and let the doctors have a look at you."

"There's nothing wrong with me that time won't heal."

"But, baby. Something might be broken."

I could hear the emotion in her voice, the tenderness of a loving grandma. I knew her heart hurt. I knew that she was keeping her rage contained for the moment.

"Nothing's broken."

Nothing was broken that could be fixed by staying in this house with this family. I would die if I didn't get out of here. I didn't need a doctor. I needed to get away. I needed to escape.

LONG INTO the night, I slid through my window and curled onto my bed. The weekend passed and come Monday, I didn't go to school. Or the day after that. A couple of times someone knocked on the front door and rang the doorbell, but I never got up to answer it and I guess neither Mom nor Trina did either.

Mike called several times. When I didn't answer my phone, he'd texted. One wrote that he'd driven by the house a few different times; even rang the doorbell once. One said that he was no longer accused of raping Trina. I'm not sure how that came about, but I was glad for him and didn't question it.

There were several calls and texts from Jess. Since she didn't have a car, it was difficult for her to get around. Our small town didn't exactly have public transportation. In fact, our one and only cab stopped service a couple of years ago. The owner of the car, Billy, died, and no one wanted to take his place.

I'm sick I finally texted to Jess. Will be out for a while

Answer ur phone NOW

Have the flu. Bad cramps. Can't talk.

I don't believe u. Call now.

Wanna see my puke as proof?

Fine. U better call me soon, tho.

K

Tomorrow

K

There were two calls from Miss J. I saw that she left a message but didn't bother to check it. She would just have to wait. And so would school. For the first time in my life, I didn't care about colleges, graduation. I didn't care about anything.

I sat at the desk in my room staring outside instead of at the computer, the blinking cursor mocking me. Mike and I were so far behind on our paper, I didn't know if we could catch up. Maybe Mr. Chambers would give us an extension. Maybe Mike was actually doing it on his own, though somehow I doubted that.

I'd done the preliminary research one night when I couldn't sleep, created an outline, even written the first page. But now nothing came to mind. I couldn't remember why we'd chosen the topic; or, to be honest, what the topic even was.

A small makeup mirror that Gran had given me for Christmas last year sat beside the computer, reflecting a face back at me that I didn't recognize; a face that was swollen, bruised, pained.

My face hurt. Bad. The slaps had left superficial bruises. One on my cheekbone, from the backhand, and one on my cheek. It was the fist punch that hurt. My jaw felt like it was slightly off center, though the entire right side of my face throbbed so bad I couldn't tell exactly where he'd hit me.

I dumped the mirror into the trash can.

It was quiet in our house and outside. That was the one thing about living in such a rural area. It could get so quiet without traffic, airplanes, and an over-abundance of people filling that silent void. Here you could hear your thoughts, whether you wanted to or not.

But today, I just didn't have the energy to do anything else so I let the quiet envelop me like an electric blanket in the high heat of a summer month; stifling me and swallowing my breaths before they even left my body.

The sound of a car reverberated off the stoic trees and bounced around like a foghorn blaring. I glanced outside to find a brown station wagon ambling up our driveway. Miss J. had come to check on me.

She pulled the car to a stop in front of the house and got out. Her brown hair was pulled into a ponytail and she wore some sort of brown scarf that looked out of place in April.

When she started toward the house, I got up and glanced in the full-length mirror that hung on the back of my door. I looked like I'd been in the boxing ring with Mike Tyson.

I yanked a brush through my hair then pulled it back into a ponytail. It was limp and greasy since I hadn't showered. I checked my teeth in the mirror, grabbed a mint on my way down the hall, and threw open the door before she could ring the bell.

"Hi" I stepped onto the porch and closed the door behind me.

"Rowan! What happened to you?" She reached out to touch my face but I moved past her and went to find Levi. He sat as far forward as the chain allowed. When I bent down to him, he didn't try to lick my cheeks, like he always did. Instead he nuzzled my shoulder and then rested his head against my arm.

"Rowan. Wait."

I looked up and shielded my eyes against the sun. It was a bright spring day, cloudless and warm.

"I'm fine," I answered to her unasked question. "The police came. Dad's gone. Who knows where? Maybe he's in jail. Maybe he's drunk in a ditch. Maybe he found another family that he likes better."

"Your father did this?"

"Yep." I sank my face into Levi's fur.

"Where's Trina? Your mother?"

I shrugged.

The humidity was high today and soon swarms of bugs, gnats and mosquitos would make being outside unbearable. I still had on my T-shirt and hoodie, despite the warmer temperatures, and I pulled the sleeves down over my hands and rubbed the backs of my arms.

"When are you planning to come back to school?"

I looked out over the yard. Even with spring rains, it was brown and patchy. It wouldn't grow green and lush. Not at all. Never had. Dad didn't put much care into it, though, so I don't know if it even had potential to be a nice yard. Guess the same could be said for our family.

"I don't know. Guess after this," and I waved my hand at my face, "heals." I shrugged. "Who knows?"

We were quiet for several minutes. She pulled a blade of grass out of the ground and tied it into a knot. She threw it aside and pulled out another. Then another. And another. Her hands, petite and unblemished, moved in smooth motion. Her brown hair was held back by a large, oval tortoise shell clip but several strands fell out around her face. It made her look young.

"How old are you?" I asked.

She glanced at me. "Twenty-five. Why?"

"You're young."

"Hmm. I'm old enough to have gone to college."

"What did you study?"

"Psychology and education."

"Cool." I started tying grass into knots too.

"I'm also working on a Master's in psychology. Going to night school."

"Busy times, huh?"

She chuckled. "It's not easy. But it's what I want to do." She touched my arm. "So I make it work."

I stared at her fingers and wondered if they'd ever hit another human. Somehow I thought not.

I tossed my blade of grass aside and picked up another one.

"I'm a testament to determination," she continued. "That we can do anything we want to if we want it bad enough."

I nodded and took her blade of grass from her fingers. Tying it into a knot, I said, "The last time my mom drove a car was a couple of days before Aidan died." If someone asked, I wouldn't be able to say why I brought up my mom's car. It had been sold ages ago. But I remember where it used to sit–right near the shed. Even before Dad sold it, it had grown rusted.

"Where did she go that day?"

Miss J. and I didn't talk about Aidan's death. The only time she'd ever directly mentioned it was last week in her office when she decided to tell me it wasn't my fault. But all the details were in my file; the same file that had followed me since the fifth grade, since I was ten. I flunked that year of school and that's when I got the file that would follow me to my high school graduation.

"I don't remember. Grocery store or somewhere. Gran had been there to watch us. Then when Mom got home, Gran left. Then Mom and Dad got into that fight."

"That fight?"

"The fight that ended with Dad leaving us, Mom going into her room and not coming out, and Aidan crying in his bed."

Something like the weight of a cinder block settled into my chest, like it did anytime I thought about my baby brother. It made it hard to breathe, but I didn't let Miss J. know that. I forced my words to be steady and strong, ignoring the pain right in my middle. I gathered all the blades and lined them up in a row. "I took care of Aidan that night."

"Did she ever come out of her room? When she heard Aidan crying?"

"She didn't come out all night."

"Where was your grandma?"

"She wasn't there."

"So no one was caring for your baby brother?"

"I was, I guess."

Miss J. already knew all of this. If not in this level of detail, then enough to get the gist. But for some reason, I was talking about it. I guess something in me wanted to.

"So, then, what happened?"

I laughed, a sound with more high pitches and lack of control than I wanted, and shook my head. Memories tumbled around inside my brain. "I was so proud. So proud that I could help." My voice choked on words I had never, not once, spoken. "I took care of Aidan. I got him a bottle. Changed him. Put him back to bed after rocking him."

I ripped up a handful of brownish grass by the roots. "And then…and then I put that damned blanket on him. I didn't cover his head. But I did put the blanket on him." I grabbed another fistful and ripped it out. "They said it was SIDS. Sudden Infant Death Syndrome, or something like that. I guess babies are never supposed to have blankets on them when they sleep. They said he'd gotten overheated, or something."

She leaned into my peripheral vision. I could sense her willing me to look at her, to see the force of conviction in her eyes, but I didn't. She continued anyway. "Rowan, Aidan's death was not your fault. You never should've been left alone with him. You were ten!"

"Yeah," I huffed. "I was ten. And have been blamed for his death ever since." Blamed by my family, and yes, by myself.

Miss J. leaned toward me. She didn't touch me but I could feel the heat from her presence. She smelled like drugstore lotion, a mix of vanilla and lavender. It was a little strong, but smelled nice anyway.

It was comforting to have her close, which I'm sure she meant it to be. But she was also too close. I held still for a few seconds but then I had to scoot away, clutching my left arm in my hand.

We sat there for a long time, a couple of feet apart. I had no more words to say to her. If she said goodbye when she got up to leave, I didn't hear her. The next thing I realized, though, was her car driving away from our home and disappearing into the sunshine.

I don't know when she expected me back at school. She had said that if you want something bad enough, you can't let anything stand in your way. I'd have to ask her what her story was one of these days. I had a feeling she would tell me the truth, even though she'd told me before that she was my counselor, not my friend; and that there were boundaries to respect. I bet this time, though, she'd tell me.

And then she'd want to know what I wanted. What did I want? Out of this home. Out of this family. I wanted to graduate high school. Go to college. Change my life…get out of this home.

Get out of this home.

chapter fourteen

THERE HAD been no sign of Mom. Her door had remained shut, against us, against the world. She hadn't even come out, that I could tell, to eat. That either meant she had sworn off food or she had a stash in her closet. The latter option was likely the case. Mom turned to junk food when her life felt out of her control, which was all the time.

Gran said she used to be petite, not quite like me, but close. Pictures of her in high school showed a smiling, thin girl with long, brown hair. In the yearbook was a picture of Mom and Dad, who were high school sweethearts. Or so Mom said. Little jabs Dad had aimed at her through the years told me that may not have been the case. Mom didn't like to talk about it so I never pushed. Dad's words lingered in my memory, though; his words comparing her to Trina. Something about *entrapping* him. Had Mom gotten pregnant on purpose?

On the morning after Miss J.'s visit, I decided to return to school and leave the catacomb that had become home. The bruises were less black and blue and more yellow and brown today. In the shower, I washed my face gently, careful not to put any pressure on my skin. Then I held up my left arm, free of bandages, to let the warm water wash over the cuts. They were healing well enough.

I knew it was wrong to cut myself. Miss J. even had a pamphlet in her bookshelf about girls who cut. And I had been so good for the past few years, not adding to the ladder of red slashes. Guess I couldn't hold on forever, though. At some point the pain of being a member of this family was bound to catch up with me.

I scrubbed the rest of my body clean, leaving my skin and scalp raw and tender. Trina's makeup bag, overflowing with cosmetics, half of which I didn't know what they were used for, sat beside the sink. I rifled through it until I found a bottle of Trina's foundation. Leaning into the bathroom mirror, I turned on all the lights, two over the mirror, one in the ceiling, and tried to apply the brown liquid. I smoothed it all over my face with my fingertips, trying to blend it around my chin. Then I reapplied a heavier layer over the bruises, patting the makeup into place.

The face looking back at me in the mirror looked like a brown ghost. But the bruises weren't visible, which to me meant goal achieved. The makeup was a little dark for my skin, but if I zipped up my hoodie all the way, no one would be able to see my neck.

I shuffled through the rest of her makeup bag and found blush, which I applied to the apples of my cheeks. I powdered my face, adding a pasty finish then a heavy coat of pinkish red lipstick.

Black eyeliner was next. I swiped it over my top and bottom lids, from one corner of my eye to the other. Then I put on several coats of black mascara. After running a comb through my hair, I teased, sprayed, teased and tousled it until I looked like the remake of an eighties rock star.

If the reflection looking back at me resembled me at all, which it didn't, I'd have cried for the little girl behind all that camouflage. But the person staring at me looked like Trina, if she had brown hair. I looked nothing like myself. And that was good. Maybe no one would recognize me at school.

There was a spot of red on my teeth so I swiped my tongue over it. For the final touch, I grabbed the bottle of perfume that Trina wore every day, even on the weekends. I spritzed my wrists, held my breath against the onslaught of scent molecules invading my nostrils, and left the bathroom as quietly as I'd entered it.

After filling Scout's bowls, I changed her litter box and slid out the front door. The sun was on the rise and it was a warm spring morning. Levi bounded around the corner and I gave him a quick hug, checked his bowls and then kissed his head.

"I'll be back later, bud."

He studied me with large round eyes that seemed too reflective. I turned away. "I'll be back soon," I said again, and hurried to the car.

I avoided the rearview mirror as I drove to school. There were two people I wanted to see and I hoped they would be at school early. I hadn't even bothered to ask Trina if she was going. In fact, we hadn't exchanged a single word in days.

But when I pulled into the school parking lot, it wasn't Mike or Miss J. that I saw. It was Christian, leaning against his car. He had a blue bandana tied around his head. On anyone else it would've looked silly. On Christian, though, it looked cool. I pulled the car in beside his and got out.

"Trina-" he started, but stopped. "Rowan?" He pushed off his car. "I thought you were Trina. You look different." He squinted until his eyes were narrow slits. "Are you okay? Where's Trina?"

I grabbed my backpack and hoisted it over my shoulder. "She's at home, I guess. Don't know. I left before she got up."

He studied my face.

"Have you seen Mike today? Is he here yet?" I asked, agitated. There were four other cars there. I didn't recognize Mike's but sometimes he caught a ride with a friend. The lot would be full in about twenty minutes and I wanted to be inside before then.

"I haven't seen him." Christian put his hand on my arm. "Rowan?"

"What?"

"Are you okay?"

I eased away from him. "I'm fine. Gotta go."

"Rowan." I could sense, more than see, him reach for me again. But I didn't linger. I darted toward the main door and slid into the school.

The halls were quiet. The only sounds were the soft hum of the air conditioner, teachers writing on chalkboards, shuffling papers, stapling. The cleaning crew was moving their large garbage cans, full of cleaning supplies, toward the maintenance closet. The men and women that made up the cleaning crew were the only foreigners that lived in our area. They were Asian, though I wasn't sure which country they were from. No one that I knew of had ever bothered to ask. Maybe I would one day.

I eased down the hall with my eyes on the floor until I came to Miss J.'s office. She was at her desk, head bent over papers. In her hand she held a red pen and was marking up some document. I watched her through the glass in the door until she looked up. Her eyes widened when she saw me. After a pause, she waved me inside.

"Rowan...Are you okay?"

I slumped into the seat across from her. "Fine. Why?"

"You look different, for one thing."

"Yeah. I thought it would be better to look like a clown than to look like I was on the losing end of a meet and greet with a pit bull."

She nodded, her eyes wide as she watched me. "Is your father back home?"

"Nah. Haven't seen him. Don't know if he'll ever come back."

"I've talked with a worker at Child Protective Services."

"About what?"

"You and Trina."

I nodded.

"You have a few different options. Different than what Trina has."

I nodded. I was almost eighteen. Trina was almost sixteen. I would be an adult soon, out on my own, even though I still had one more year of high school.

"Yep. Lucky me."

"Have you thought about living on your own?"

I shrugged again, already growing tired of this conversation. So I changed the topic. "I did get asked to the Prom."

"By whom?"

I clamped my lips together and flipped my hand in the air.

"Are you going to go?"

Would Mike even still want to take me?

Miss J. was quiet for several moments, opening that space in time for thoughts to swarm in my head like unsettled, irritated bees. What would happen to Trina? Maybe she'd stay at the house with Mom. She could take care of her baby while taking care of Mom. God knew it wouldn't be the other way around. And if Dad didn't return, it wouldn't matter whether Trina left.

Dad, who knew what would happen to him. He could get his own place and wallow in his misery over what might've been if the baby hadn't died. Or better than that, if Mom hadn't gotten pregnant in high school, *trapping* him into a marriage he didn't want. I'd have to find out the truth about that situation. Maybe Gran would tell me.

"I'll figure out my options later," I said. "I'm sure we'll be getting a visit from CPS soon and I'll cross that bridge when I get to it. But now, I need to graduate. Then I need to get into college. I've missed a few days with this." I rolled my eyes and pointed to my face. "But it shouldn't affect anything."

I pulled out the red lipstick that I'd taken from Trina's makeup bag and smeared on another layer. Miss J. watched me, blinking several times like there was something in her eye. With a sigh, she pulled a folder from the corner of her desk. After flipping through a few pages, she shut it again.

"Just make sure you don't miss anymore. And be on time."

I slumped a little lower in the chair. "I know. I will. From now on I'll be here every day, on time. With Trina or without."

"Okay. You have a test in trig. Have you studied?"

I gritted my teeth. I'd forgotten about that and trig was not my best subject. "Yes." I eased the waxy stick in and out of the smooth black tube. The bright, creamy color was mesmerizing.

"How do they make lipstick?" I ran the pad of my finger over the slanted tip. "It's really pretty."

"Rowan." Her voice was full of things I didn't want to hear: warnings, worries, threats.

The bell rang.

"Gotta go. Thanks." I grabbed my backpack and headed toward the door.

"Rowan?"

"Hmm?" I turned.

"Take off some of that makeup. At least take off the lipstick. You don't want to look like someone you're not."

I grabbed a tissue from a table beside the door and left. I darted into the bathroom before anyone could see me; lipstick in one hand, tissue in the other. The halls were filling up with students now and the bathroom mirrors were already occupied by girls reapplying the makeup they'd just applied at home.

I slid into a stall and used toilet paper to wipe off the lipstick. Then I reapplied it, looking into the reflective silver surface of the bag hook. It was probably uneven but I didn't care. For some reason that thought made me smile.

Back out in the hall, I kept my head down and made my way through two hallways until I came to my locker. The scent of old books and erasers hit me when I opened it. I really should get an air freshener. I leaned in, searching for my chem book when a familiar voice spoke near my ear.

"There you are!" Mike touched my shoulder. "Hey."

I didn't want to turn; didn't want him to see me.

He tapped my shoulder. "Rowan?"

"Hmm?"

He leaned around. "Look at me." He put a finger under my chin. At first I resisted the pull of his finger but then, finally, I let him turn my face.

"Oh my God. Rowan?"

I didn't know if he was horrified by the makeup or the bruises.

"Rowan, what happened?"

He put both of his hands on my face. His brows were creased, lips slightly parted. I inhaled his scent, letting it fill my insides. For the first time in days, I felt *alive*.

"Are you okay?"

I blinked several times. "I'm fine." But I wasn't and tears spilled out from my lids and slid over my brown makeup. Mike dropped his hands from my face and wrapped his arms around me.

My arms wound around his back. I inhaled deeply and imagined my tears leaving brown streaks down his white shirt. His heartbeat was strong against my cheek. I counted each beat until I felt my own heartbeat's rhythm merge with his.

I exhaled.

chapter fifteen

THE WARNING bell clanged and students hurried all around us. Mike handed me a tissue from his pocket and I dabbed at my eyes. The tissue was smeared with black.

"I have to get to class. I have a trig test later and haven't studied."

"Here." He pulled the tissue from my hands and wiped my eyes for me. "Rowan?"

"Hmm?"

"Why are you wearing so much makeup? I thought you were Trina."

Was the makeup so blaring people didn't notice our hair color was different? Our bodies?

"Gotta hide the bruises somehow."

"What bruises?" He grasped my chin and lifted it up. The fluorescent bulbs overhead hurt my eyes and small black dots peppered my vision. Guess he had only been horrified by the makeup. What would he think now?

"Rowan, what happened?" His words quivered. "Who did this to you?"

I pulled away. "I gotta go, Mike. I have to get to class."

He put his hands on my shoulders, stopping me. "Rowan," he said through clenched teeth. "Who did this to you?"

"Dad." He released me this time when I pulled away. Over my shoulder, I said, "It's okay if you don't want to take me to the Prom. I know I'm not the kind of girl you'd want to take home to your mom."

Before he could answer, I pulled my hair over my face and darted down the hall. I eased into my seat just as the tardy bell rang.

Mr. Chambers was passing out papers and when he laid the white paper on my desk, my heart nearly fell to my toes. A quiz. A quiz so soon after a test? How could I have forgotten? I swallowed past the leaden lump in my throat and willed myself not to cry. Of course, I hadn't been to school in days. How was I supposed to know?

One failed quiz–now. One failed test–later. All in one day. And our biology report? Nothing. I'd done nothing on that. I bit my lip to keep from bolting out of my chair, jumping out the window and running until I fell off the face of the earth.

Beads of sweat broke out on my forehead and I envisioned the brown makeup oozing down my face like a waterfall. Soon it would be a puddle on my quiz and there would be nowhere to put my answers. Not that I knew many of them anyway. The pencil shook in my hand. My heart muscles clenched and I grasped my chest. I couldn't get enough air to fill my lungs.

Counting to myself, I tried to force deep breaths, to make my chest expand and fill my lungs with air. I tried to make the pencil, held tight between my fingers, stop shaking. I tried to make the black letters on the white paper merge into words I actually understood.

But when the words on the page whirled into a mix of black dots, I jumped up.

"I can't do this." I stumbled up the aisle toward the door.

"Rowan?" Mr. Chambers looked up from his desk.

"I've gotta go." I pushed out the door and into the hallway.

"Rowan!"

The door slammed shut behind me. I fell against the lockers, gasping for breath.

"Are you okay?" Mr. Chambers slid to a halt in front of me. "Rowan, what's wrong?" His face bent to level with mine. "Do I need to call the nurse or 911? Rowan, speak to me. Now."

I shook my head and gulped. "I'm not prepared for that quiz."

His eyes scanned my face. I could feel it. I turned to the side.

"Rowan, has someone hit you?" He tried to move in front of me again but I walked away.

"Yes. But my guidance counselor knows." I faced him full on. "I'm not prepared for the quiz." I knew my bruises were no longer masked with the makeup; that it had melted off. He would see them as plain as the color of my eyes.

"Of course, Rowan, you can make it up. You just let me know when you're ready."

A ball filled my throat, making it difficult to speak the words that I needed to. But I managed to choke out, "Thank you," before I swallowed painfully. I turned before my eyes would spill over again.

"Rowan?"

"Yes?" I glanced over my shoulder.

"Everything will be okay. You'll see. Everything will be just fine."

The ball erupted from somewhere deep inside my chest, forcing waves of despair through my body. I ran down the hall, heaving, and ducked into the bathroom before he could see my tears.

I slammed the stall door shut and fumbled with the lock. Then I slid to the floor and cried-loud, hiccupping crying that echoed off the tiled walls. With shaky fingers, I reached into my pocket and pulled out the thin, familiar steel and yanked up my shirt sleeve.

WHEN I reemerged some time later, the quietness of the bathroom was overwhelming. I filled my lungs with several long, deep pulls. On shaky feet, I walked to the basin and ran the cold water. With hands white with soapy suds, I washed my face. Soap ran into my eyes, making them sting like I'd washed with vinegar. But

I didn't stop until I'd washed my face twice, tears from the soap mixing with the water.

Then I rinsed several times. My eyes were puffy and red but there were no remnants of the black liner. There was no evidence of the lipstick or the blush, or the brown liquid that had tried in vain to mask the evidence of what it was like to be a member of my family.

THE REST of the day passed in oblivion. Someone must've talked to my trig teacher. Before I even sat down in my seat, Mrs. Sanders pulled me aside and told me that today she wasn't letting me test. She wanted me to go into the library and find a quiet place to study. I could take the test next week.

At first, I didn't understand her. She wasn't making me take the test? Then she gently turned me toward the door and gave the slightest of pushes until I left the classroom and went to the library.

The rest of the day passed in a haze. I know I went to the rest of my classes because, by the end of the day, I had a backpack full of homework and a planner full of assignments. But if someone asked me a single thing about any of my classes, or lunch, the only single event I'd be able to pinpoint that had happened was that Mike had held me in his arms. In fact, I could still feel his warmth. I wasn't surprised to find him leaning against my car when I left the building at the end of the day.

"Hey," I managed. I searched for something normal to say. I settled on, "No practice today?"

"Yeah, there is. But I'm not going."

"Why not?" I glanced up at him. Did the bruises make me disfigured? Ugly? Why didn't I leave that makeup on? At least then it would've looked more like I was trying too hard to look like Trina than it was that I was covering up something.

"I'm not going to practice today. I need to talk to you."

"Need to talk to me?"

"Yes, you. Why did your dad do this to you?"

I glanced around the parking lot. No one was looking at us but I felt self-conscious anyway.

"I'm not going anywhere until you've answered me." His words were like concrete and steel nestled in soft, warm down.

I nodded, letting a breath ease out of my nose. "My dad knows about Christian. He went out, got drunk, then came home."

"And did this to you?"

I nodded. "Yep. Something like that."

"Well, why did he hit you if Trina was the one who got herself pregnant?"

I was quiet for several minutes. Did he know about Aidan? It was a small town. Word got around. It may have happened seven years ago, but that didn't mean anything.

I shook my head. "Mike, I can't get into it now."

"Try. Please."

I touched the bruise on my cheek and pushed my finger into its center, sending a shot of pain over my face. "My brother died years ago. And my dad, none of us, has ever been the same."

"Oh, man. That's tough. But it doesn't explain why he hit you when Trina comes home pregnant?"

I wanted to tell him to quit asking. *Don't push me on this.*

"Rowan, why?" he persisted. "Why did he do this to you?"

Then, against my will, I answered. "To sum it up, he died because he got overheated when he was asleep. I, I…" then I blurted it out, "I put the blanket on him that made him too hot."

"What? Rowan, oh my God." He pulled me against him.

As he held me, I could feel his muscles go from comforting to tense. "I'll kill him."

I stepped back. "What? Who?"

"Your dad."

"Mike, he's not even home."

"Is he coming back?"

I shrugged. "I assume so. Why?"

"No."

"What?"

"No. You are not going back there if he is coming home."

I stared at him for a long time. There was a thread of irritation that wove through my brain at his words. Who did he think he was, telling me where I could or couldn't go? But larger than that thread was a wave of emotion–a mixture of relief, happiness, a warm feeling that made my skin tingle. He didn't want me to return home. Did he care about me that much?

"Yes." He crossed his arms over his chest. He kicked his backpack away from his feet. Leaning down into my face, his eyes level with mine, he said, "Yes."

"Yes, what?"

"Yes, I do care about you that much. And you know what else?"

I shook my head.

"You're beautiful."

I burst into tears.

"YOU DO?" I asked about his first question. Then I asked, "I am?" to his second. My bag slid off my shoulder and fell to the ground.

He pulled me to him again. If I could crawl inside of him and stay there forever, I would.

"I care about you that much," he said into my hair. I was so glad I'd showered that morning. "Rowan, why can't you believe that?"

"But why? Why would you want to go out with a girl like me?"

"A girl like you? Rowan," he said, and lifted my chin. "You are amazing. You're beautiful. Smart. Got a nice ass." He smiled and I couldn't stop the melting of my heart, even as I punched him in the arm. "I don't know." He ran a hand through his hair. "There's just something about you."

"Something about me?" I tried to lure his words from his lips and immerse them into my brain, in a place where I may actually be able to believe what he said.

"Yes." He bent toward me and pressed his lips against mine. I leaned into his large body, willing him to keep me afloat, desperate for his strength to help me maneuver through my life. His touch was gentle, reassuring, only slightly tense still. So sweet my muscles almost gave up the strength to hold me. I put my arms around his neck and let my lips part. I didn't care who was watching. When Mike kissed me, nothing else in the world mattered.

Somewhere in the distance, I heard catcalls and whistles. It was probably the soccer team, watching their teammate make out in the parking lot. I didn't care, though, as long as I was the one making out with him.

One hand cupped my face while we kissed and the other one slid down to the small of my back, sending shots of electricity straight through every cell in my body. I think I whimpered. Or sighed. Or moaned. Or all three.

After several moments, he broke the kiss. "Come with me."

"Come with you? Where?" I didn't want to leave the warmth of his arms or the power of his kiss.

"I want you to meet my mom."

"Your mom?" I choked. "Why?" Meet his mom? With these bruises? Not an option.

"Because she's a great woman. I think you'll like her. I know she'll like you."

I'm sure she was a nice woman but I seriously doubted she wanted her son to bring home a girl who gets beaten up by her father.

"I caught a ride with Jason to school this morning, so if you don't mind, we can take your car. I'll tell you how to get there."

Jason was one of Mike's neighbors and fellow soccer player. At one point, right before Paul, Jess had had a crush on him. But when she hooked up with Paul, there seemed to be no looking back.

"I don't know, Mike. I'll give you a ride home, but I don't know about meeting your mom. I'm not exactly at my best."

"My mom will love you." He pulled away and grabbed his bag as if the discussion was over. He walked around to the passenger side of my car. "Shall we?"

I didn't move. I wasn't up for a *meet the parents*. "I'll drop you off at home, but I can't meet your mom, Mike. Not today."

He smiled, flashing the white teeth and dimples that sent a pierce straight through my heart. I returned his smile. I'd do whatever he asked of me at that moment. With a sigh, I slid into the driver's seat, tossing my bag into the back.

"Rowan!" I jumped as Jess started banging on the window.

Clutching my chest, I rolled down the window.

"My God, Ro! What happened? Who did this to you? I knew something was wrong!"

I sighed. "I know. I look awful." I let the words tumble out of my mouth. "It doesn't hurt. No really"

"Ro? Who. Did. This. To. You?" Jess's teeth were clenched and her eyes were so wild, I leaned away.

Only then did she see Mike.

"Mike?"

There was a flash of accusation across her face and I said hurriedly, "It was Dad. Dad did this. Can I call you later?"

"You're not going back there are you? You can come and stay with me instead."

"Jess, that's sweet, but you know that wouldn't work."

Mike leaned forward. "No. She's coming to my house."

My head whipped around. "What? I'm not meeting your mom today."

"Yes, you are. And you'll stay there. She'll insist."

"What?" I sputtered.

"That's a great idea." Jess leaned into the car, shoving her glasses up her nose. I could smell her citrus-scented lotion.

"What?" My brain was a muddle of confusion.

My phone started to ring. With a huff, feeling my decisions were slowly being taken away from me, and not being sure I minded, I fished the phone out of my back pocket and glanced down at the caller ID. It was Gran.

"Go to the hospital," she said. "It's Trina."

"What is it?" Mike whispered. "What's wrong?"

"Gran, what happened? Is she okay?"

"Just go. I gotta run. I'll see you there." She hung up.

"I've...I've gotta go. Something's wrong with Trina." I flipped my phone shut and looked at Jess then at Mike. "I have to go to the hospital."

"I'll go with you," Mike said.

"I'm coming too." Jess jumped into the backseat as I threw the car into *drive* and slammed my foot on the gas.

"Did she say what's wrong?" Mike asked, as I peeled out of the parking lot.

"I guess it's the baby. I...I don't know."

"Who was it on the phone?"

"My grandma."

I drove through town until the hospital loomed before us; a red brick monstrosity that always reminded me of what a mental hospital should look like.

I found a space near the emergency entrance. We jumped out of the car. Mike came around to my side as I locked the doors and as we walked toward the building, he grasped my hand. I leaned into him.

The muscles of his arm were hard against the side of my cheek. If he did, in fact, care for me, he'd have to have more than just muscles, though. Baggage followed me. Damage. Wounds. Mike squeezed my hand like he could hear my thoughts.

Jess kept in step beside me, not touching me, but keeping close enough to me that if I stumbled, I knew she'd catch me.

We passed through the automatic glass doors and into the brightly lit entrance. We almost ran into Gran, pacing near the reception area.

"Gran? What's wrong?" I put my hand on her arm and shook gently. She seemed entranced as she stared at me through vacant eyes.

"Rowan, Trina tried to kill herself."

chapter sixteen

"WHAT?" AIR seeped out of my chest.

Gran's eyes were swollen and red. She took my hand. Hers was dry and I could feel the loose skin wrinkling against my palm.

"She tried to kill herself. She took some pills. I'm not sure what."

Trina? Took pills? Tried to kill herself? Not Trina. Not my baby sister.

"When?" Mike asked.

Gran was quiet, like she wasn't going to answer. She was staring at Mike.

"Gran, Mike Anderson. Mike, Gran."

They both nodded, not exactly the moment for pleasantries. If Gran put two-and-two together and realized this was the *Mike* that Trina had made so many accusations against, I didn't know.

"And you know Jess."

Jess gave her a quick hug.

Gran pulled in a big breath and answered Mike's question. "We're not sure. Your mother found her sometime this morning. She called me around noon and told me to meet them here."

"Is she going to be okay?" Mike asked this question softly, leaning toward Gran, as if he didn't want me to hear it. Or the answer.

Gran looked like she had aged ten years, with wrinkles grown deeper, hair a shade whiter, and a sorrow in her gaze that only came from a life of heartache.

"We don't know yet. They've pumped her stomach. But she took a lot of pills. And your mom thinks she maybe have drank."

"Drank?" Jess asked.

"There was an empty vodka bottle in her trash can. I don't know how much had been in it or if she even had any. But it seems like she did."

"Oh, man." Mike rubbed his chin. "What can we do?"

"Just wait." Gran gave a small, sympathetic smile that in no way spread further than her mouth.

"Where's Mom?" I managed to find my voice.

"In the back. There's another waiting room back there, for immediate family."

"Dad?"

She shook her head as her eyes filled. "There's been no sign of him. Your mom called his cell but he didn't pick up."

"The baby?" I choked.

"I don't know, honey. I just don't know."

"Okay." Images of Trina's face loomed before me: her as a chubby-cheeked toddler, with golden ringlets and bright blue eyes; her as a ballerina for Halloween when she was five. Her, the first time she got mad at me, when she was seven and I wouldn't let her watch an 'R' rated movie while Mom was at a doctor's appointment. Her, at eight, watching me the morning after Aidan's death. Something in her changed that day. Something discreet and hidden, but as palpable to me as my own heartbeat. Things hadn't been the same since.

And now she was in a hospital, after a teenage pregnancy and a suicide attempt. What had happened to us? Why did this happen? Hadn't we suffered enough?

No matter what had changed in Trina, she was my sister. And she needed me.

"I have to see her," I said hurriedly. "I can help. She needs me. Let me go back there." My body convulsed with my ache. I could make it all better. I had to get to her.

"I'm immediate family. I can go back there." I hurried to the counter. "Excuse me but my sister is back there. I want to see her." I wiped my eyes with the back of my hand.

"What's her name, sweetie?"

"Trina. Trina Slone. She's hurt and she needs me. I'm her sister."

Mike rubbed my back and Gran had her hand on mine, staring at the administrator. I could feel Jess standing behind me.

"Can she visit her sister?" Gran asked.

"Let me check her status. Is there a family member back there already?"

"Yes," Gran answered. "Her mother."

"Only one person can be back there at a time. I'll check in with your mother and the doctors. I'll see if I can't find out some information for you." She tried to smile, tried to show me a reassuring expression; but there was something in her eyes, a foreboding, a sense of doom. Maybe I imagined it.

Maybe I'd never see my sister alive again.

AT SOME point I was led to the waiting room. I slumped into a chair in the corner and let my head fall against the wall. With eyes closed, I heard more than saw Gran, Jess and Mike sit near me. They talked in hushed tones as I thought about Trina's face, so sweet and beautiful underneath the layers of makeup. Why would she try to kill herself? Was our life so bad?

The simple answer was *yes*. Our lives were bad. But would I ever consider killing myself?

I hadn't. Not even when Dad's cold, accusing eyes followed me everywhere I turned. Not when Mom, unable to cope, retreated into her depression-induced stupor and rarely left it. Not when Dad's fist flew into my face and landed me home in bed and missing school.

I closed my eyes, eager to check-out. But the hospital was full of conversations, beeps, blaring lights and intercom calls to staff. The waiting room was crowded with all sorts of people, all with their own concerns, dramas, and pains. A group near us talked in such loud voices, it sounded like they were using an intercom. One of their loved ones was in the ER because of a gunshot wound he'd gotten while hunting. If I even paid half attention, I would leave there knowing every detail of the wounded hunter's story.

Opening my eyes, or ears, wasn't an option, though. I didn't want to see, or hear, the world around me. Not when that world might never include my little sister again. Even if I hated her; even if we never talked again because of her lies and her accusations, the world needed her in it.

She was strong. She would make it out. I didn't know how many pills she'd taken. Or how much vodka she'd drank. But she would make it through.

When Aidan died, he'd taken with him the hope and optimism of our family. Not that we were ever a perfect family or ever destined to become one. But there was hope. And there was light. When he died, all of that went with him. The only thing left in his wake was blame. And guilt. And irreversible despair. Is that what led Trina to this point?

Was I to blame for her death too if she died?

Mike was rubbing my arm with light, gentle strokes. His touch was soothing and sweet, reassuring as much as anything could be at that moment. Then he trailed his fingers over my hand and rubbed across the mounds of my knuckles. When he was done with that, he traced each of my fingers with his.

What was he thinking? Sitting here with his beat-up semi-girl-friend, maybe-still Prom date, in a hospital because her crazy sister tried to kill herself after getting pregnant and kicked out of the house. How could he take someone like me home to his mom? How could he want to take me to Prom?

The question formed on my lips. I opened my eyes and found him staring at me. And I stared back at him, wishing he could read my thoughts. Wishing he could understand that I understood he was too good for me and I would let him go.

At first his brows creased and his lips parted, like he was going to ask me what I was thinking. Then he squinted and leaned toward me, ever so slightly. The intensity behind those green eyes made my breath catch in my throat, but I couldn't say anything. I tried to open my mouth, but he put a finger over my lips and shook his head, his eyes never leaving mine.

Why are you with me? My eyes implored.

Because I care for you. Nothing will deter that. Not this. Not anything else, his gaze said back to me. His perfect lips broke into a smile. Not a jubilant, excited smile. Just a very small, very slight smile that didn't mask the concern behind his gaze, or the severity of the moment. But that slight gesture managed to answer my unasked questions and reassure me. My head fell toward him. He wrapped his arm around my shoulders and held me close. I felt a fleeting moment of peace.

"Rowan?"

I opened my eyes. Mom stood before me.

"Mom?" I was shocked by the child-like sound to my voice. "Is she okay? Is Trina okay?"

Mom started to cry and Gran stood beside her, rubbing the back of her shoulder.

"Mom? Gran? Is Trina okay?"

Mom collapsed and I caught her before she hit the floor. My knees buckled under her weight, but Mike grabbed us both and helped me support her while Jess held Mom by the shoulders.

"Mom?" I asked into her hair. "Answer me."

"I don't know." She struggled to speak. "I just don't know."

My sobs mirrored my mother's gasp for gasp.

"The baby?" I choked.

She shook her head. "Gone," she whispered. "She lost the baby."

Numbness oozed over me. How was I supposed to feel about that? Were we glad it happened? Sad? Relieved? Did it matter at all if my sister didn't make it?

I pushed against Mom to get her to stand up on her own. Her weight was too much for me, even with Mike's help. Instead of staying on her own feet, she turned and fell into Gran who had to plant her feet like a wrestler in order to hold her. Gran stroked her hair like she was a small child.

I watched them for several long moments, a mother consoling her child. In many ways my mom was still a child. She wasn't the one who consoled us. Trina and I consoled her in the wake of Aidan's death; in the aftermath of Dad's rages. She was still very much the child in her mother's arms. Did she not realize that we also needed a mother like that? That the mother we needed was supposed to be her?

Our home was no place for a baby. No place at all. It was best that this baby wasn't introduced into our lives. There was deep heartache and not enough love. Besides, without the baby, Trina could stay at home. Maybe Dad wouldn't return. Maybe he would.

I stumbled to the counter. "Can I see my sister now?"

The administrator glanced at Mom. She was huddled in a chair, clutching her large stomach, with Gran rubbing her back.

"Sure sweetie. I'm sure she'll be happy to see you. For just a minute, though. She's awake but very, very weak. You can see her for no more than five minutes."

"Okay." I turned to Mike and Jess.

Both nodded at the same time. "We'll be right here." Mike pointed to the spot where he and Jess stood. I had little doubt they would still be there, in exactly that spot, when I walked back out of those ivory doors. That simple thought gave me the strength to walk through them and to go to my sister.

THE NURSE led me down the white hall, and I blinked against the glaring light. We entered the emergency area with rows of curtained cubicles. Some curtains were open, but most were closed. A man was shuffling toward us, his old, withered hand clutching an IV. We paused to let him pass before turning down another curtained hall until she finally stopped.

"We're going to keep her for a few days to make sure she is stable. Her room will be ready soon, but she'll have to stay here until it is." She lifted the curtain. "She's very weak and lightly sedated. Just take a few minutes, okay?"

"Okay." My throat was dry and scratchy.

She placed a hand on my shoulder and smiled. "Your sister will be fine."

She waved me forward. There was one narrow bed with silver guardrails. Trina's small feet lifted the thin blanket. The television was on but the sound was muted.

Silently, I eased around the curtain, letting it fall shut behind me. Her name was on the tip of my tongue. *Trina…Sis…*and all the pet names I'd ever had for her when we were little. *Pumpkin butter…Billy goat*, because she could never get enough of Gran's homemade apple pies.

But none of these words left my mouth. All I could do was stare at my baby sister. Something kept me from speaking. Like if she saw me before she heard my voice, she wouldn't be resistant to seeing me. But she had to know I was there, even though she hadn't looked at me. I was standing just two feet from the bottom of her bed.

The skin of her face, neck and exposed arms looked ashen. She seemed smaller in the bed, as if this whole ordeal had sucked away actual years from her body. Her blonde curls were matted and flat.

Neither of us spoke for several minutes. I resisted the urge to crawl into the narrow bed beside her. For some reason, I didn't think that would be welcome.

Finally, she spoke. "I lost the baby. Dad will be happy."

"I know." I cleared my throat and took a step closer. She was right that Dad would be happy; or if not happy, then less likely to throw her out. That issue was taken care of. Even if Dad did decide to return to us; which how likely that was, I didn't know.

"Why did you try to kill yourself?" My voice cracked and I cleared my throat again.

If I asked her what show was on the television, I doubted she'd be able to tell me. Her silence was heavy and I almost reached for the remote to turn up the volume, to add some buffer.

"It just seemed like the right answer."

"Trina, how could you think that? That being *dead* would be better than living?"

Without moving her head, her eyes settled on my face. What I saw sent chills straight to the deepest part of my heart. I don't know exactly what she was feeling, but the look in her eyes left me in a dark, black place. If that was the place where she was herself, no wonder she wanted to leave it.

"Isn't being dead better than living? What do we have to live for, Rowan?" Her voice was emotionless. "What do we have to live for?" She looked away.

"Trina, you're only fifteen. You can stay in school. Go to college. That'll get you out of here. That's what I'm going to try to do."

She laughed a humorless, dead sound. "Yeah. I'll do that. After I figure out how to pass the subjects I'm failing."

"Which subjects? I can help." My voice rose with hope.

"I got kicked off the squad. It seems being pregnant doesn't jive with cheerleading."

She didn't realize she'd be kicked off the squad if she got pregnant? Was she serious?

"Never mind about the squad. If you're failing, you need to be studying instead." Miss J. would be proud to hear these words tumble out of my mouth.

"Oh, please," Trina snorted. "I'm not going to college. I'm not going anywhere but back to that house until some no good guy comes along and wants to marry me. Maybe I'll get knocked-up again, like Mom did, so the guy will be forced to marry me. Just like Dad was. Then I'll leave and move to his house. Have his kids. Cook his meals. Become depressed and unhappy, and fat, just like Mom." Her eyes were full but her cheeks stayed dry. "That's all that waits for me. And honestly, I don't see that it's worth it."

In one step, I was at her bedside with her hand in mine. "So it's true? Mom got pregnant just so Dad would marry her? How do you know?"

Trina's eyes dried in an instant, replaced with icy hardness. "They got in a fight one night when you weren't there. Last week." Her words were toneless, as if they held no emotion. From the look on her face, they didn't. "He kept yelling at her for getting knocked-up when they were in high school. I don't even think they were dating. He said something about drinking, Mom cornering him, and the next thing he knew, she was pregnant and his dad was forcing him to skip college and marry her. That's why he joined the Army right out of high school. It was the perfect job—he could earn the income to take care of his little wife and his unwanted child," which was me, "yet still be away from her. He told her he hated her. That he always had. Just like he's always hated us."

Trina hadn't spoken so many words to me in years. Maybe it was the sedation, loosening the walls built in her mind. Maybe it was the fact that she felt she had nothing to live for so she might as well let all those words out into the universe.

But I couldn't wrap my mind around what she was saying. I knew Mom and Dad had a bad relationship, but I didn't realize that there had never been any love there; that Mom had gotten pregnant on purpose? Were they never even a couple? That would at least explain why he didn't care for me and Trina. He'd never wanted us in the first place. But what about Aidan? He'd wanted him.

Trina seemed to follow the stream of words in my head because she continued. "It was a very enlightening conversation. You should've been there. Dad had a lot to say. He also blamed her for getting pregnant with me. He was going to leave her. His own father was dead so he felt no obligation to stay married. And that she got pregnant with me to make it harder to leave a wife and *two* children. Harder than leaving a wife and one."

Trina stared at the television like she was reading from a script.

"He told her, over and over, that I was no good, just like her. That I'd gotten knocked-up in high school, just like her. The only difference was there was no way in hell that he would force *that loser* to marry me."

Trina's skin felt alien, yet familiar, all at the same time. I was so glad she didn't pull away. I needed to feel her closeness as she spilled these devastating secrets. A tear finally escaped. It ran out of the corner and made a path over her cheek, toward her ear. With a whisper touch, I wiped it away.

"Aidan would've been the one thing to bring us together. Do you know that? He would've been the only thing that could have changed our lives. But he's dead. All because of that stupid blanket. Dad said so. He said that there was a chance after Aidan came. A chance that he could love us, love us all. But she'd blown that because she left the baby to your care,"

My heart turned stony, frigid. "It wasn't my fault." The words were spoken, but were they heard? Could Trina hear me? That it wasn't my fault? Could I hear myself?

"No, you may not have killed him outright. But you did kill him. You're the reason Mom can't get out of bed; the reason Dad hates us. We were on the right track. Until you decided to play *mommy* and be the *big girl*." Trina crooked her fingers in the air at the last words.

"You're so selfish. Everything is about you. You couldn't ask for help that day. You wanted to be the big kid, didn't you, Rowan? And now look. Our brother's dead. Our dad hates us. Our family is a mess. And it's all because of you."

chapter seventeen

HER WORDS were like lethal darts, aimed right at my heart. Was she serious? She thought it was my pride that made me put that blanket on Aidan? That had me making his bottle and changing his diaper? I wanted to show I was a *big kid?*

"Yeah, that's right," she sneered, as if I had spoken those thoughts. "All you had to do was call Gran. Or even knock on Mom's door until she opened it and came out to get him. But, no," she sang in her mocking tone, "big sister Rowan had to act like she could take care of everything. And then guess what, she *ruined* everything."

Her lips hardened. "Now, there's no hope. It's done. Everything is done. Lost. Gone. We had one chance to be a happy family. And that chance is gone."

The skin on her hand went cold, so cold beneath my own; as if the warmth of life left her completely. Her chest still followed the rise and fall of life, but her hand held none of that energy.

There was no hope for our family. I knew that. When a family is built on nothing but disdain and regrets, there is no way that family can survive. Can it? But I knew the answer. The answer was *no.* Trina was right. We'd had one chance at happiness and I'd blown it with that stupid blanket. I'd blown our family's only chance.

I dropped her hand and darted out of the room. She didn't call after me, or if she did, I didn't hear her. I ran down the hall, past the nurse's station and the nurses. Past a couple of doctors. Past people dressed in regular old clothes and patients walking around in their revealing hospital gowns, pulling IV stands beside them.

I ran into the waiting room. I didn't look for Gran. Or Mike, who was standing exactly where I left him. Or Jess, who was standing right in the middle of the waiting room, like a tall, cherry-haired, black-clad obelisk.

I hurled myself through the doors and into a blanket of rain that only added to the moisture that stained my cheeks.

"Rowan!" Jess yelled.

I didn't stop.

"Rowan!" Mike yelled.

A hand grabbed my arm and yanked me to a halt. "Rowan! Look at me!" It was Mike. Rain poured over us in sheets, like the despair inside our hearts wasn't enough.

My chest hurt too bad to breathe. I couldn't pull air into my body, even though it screamed for it. I doubled over. Mike caught me in his arms as Jess ran up to us.

"Rowan, what is it? What happened?" Jess stroked my back.

Mike held me to his chest as my body convulsed.

"Go away," I said. "Let me go."

"What?" he asked. "What did you say?"

"What?" Jess asked, but I ignored her. It was Mike I needed to talk to.

His handsome features were morphed by his concern, making him no less handsome, but more like a grown-up with real grown-up problems.

"Let me go. I'm not good for you."

His hands wrapped around my upper arms, holding me up. "Why are you saying this? Rowan, tell me what's going on!"

I tried to wrench free. He saw much goodness in me. And he seemed to be the one person I didn't want to disappoint.

"No. It's over."

He shook me. "No, it's not over. I'm not going to let you do this to yourself. You are not your sister."

"No, I'm not. But I'm no good for you." I blinked against the onslaught of rain. "I'm no good for you, Mike. You need someone you can be proud to take home to your mom."

He loosened his grip just enough for me to pull away. I stumbled back several feet and wiped my face with my sleeve. It did no good against the rain, though.

"Why are you doing this, Rowan? I don't understand."

"I'm toxic, Mike. You deserve better."

Jess tried to follow me, but I held up a hand and shook my head. She slid to a stop, a puddle of rain sloshing over the toe of her black steel-toed boots.

I grabbed my keys out of my pocket. "Gran will give you a ride. I gotta go."

Mike reached out. "No."

I didn't let him touch me. "I can't take you down with me."

His face morphed into a myriad of emotions I didn't take the time to decipher. I watched him for a few seconds more before I bolted to my car. Without looking back, I peeled out of the parking lot and left Mike and Jess standing there, staring after me. His hands were held out in front of him, like he was pleading for something. I didn't wait to hear what it was.

"TRINA TRIED to kill herself." I stumbled into the car lot.

"What?" Dan hurried toward me. "Rowan, what are you talking about? What happened?"

My wet soles slipped on the tile but Dan caught me.

"You're soaked. Where have you been?"

He tried to pull back and look at me but I wouldn't let him. He would be my life raft. Dan would be the answer: he would help get me out of my home. I couldn't wait until I left for college. And I couldn't afford to live on my own before that.

"Marry me."

"What? Rowan, again, I have to ask, what are you talking about?"

He managed to get ahold of my arms and pushed me away from him. He was wearing his raincoat, so he must've just had a customer. His thinning hair was still wet and I could smell cigarette smoke on his breath.

"I…I think we should get married. You want to go out, right? Let's just get married. Now. Today."

How could he argue with that? He could marry a young gal and I could get away from my family. It was perfect.

"You're talking nonsense." He dropped my arms and stepped away.

I closed the space between us. "No, I'm not. You've been chasing me around here for the past several months all but begging me to go out with you. I can do one better. Let's get married. I'll forge my parents' signature."

He shook his head. "Whoa, Rowan. We're not getting married. You're *seventeen*!"

"I can forge Mom's signature. She's so out of it, she'll never know. Then we'll be married, I'll turn eighteen, and everything will be great."

Words and ideas tumbled out of my mouth in waves. Couldn't he see the solution in this plan? Couldn't he see how *important* it was?

His face paled and he took several quick strides, putting the counter between us.

"Rowan, did something else happen?"

I leaned over the counter, eyes wide and earnest. "It's perfect. You're getting old. You need to be married. I can marry you! Today!" My voice was loud, squeaky.

"You're talking crazy. We're not getting married." He seemed angry now, his eyes slits of aggravation.

I hurried around the counter and threw my arms around his neck. I lifted to my toes so I could reach his lips. And I kissed him.

He shoved me off. I stumbled but caught myself on the wall.

"Rowan." His voice full of warnings and sirens.

The wind whipped through the trees outside. The lights flickered off but then almost immediately came back on.

The door flew open. "Is Rowan here?" It was Jess, soaking wet and wild-eyed. "Rowan!" She rushed toward me. "Are you okay?"

"I'm *fine*."

Jess yanked out her phone and her long, slim fingers flew through a text. "I'm texting Mike. He's on his way. We have something to tell you."

As if on cue, Mike burst through the door. "Rowan? My God, Rowan." He pulled me to him and his iron-strong arms wrapped around me.

"Rowan." He dropped down to look me in the eye. "It's a lie. It's all a lie. You didn't kill Aidan."

"Huh?" I stammered. His features were awash with rain and he blinked several times.

"It's a lie, Rowan. You didn't kill your brother."

Silence fell into the room like a heavy curtain, drawn at the end of a show.

"What?" I asked.

Mike scanned our faces in turn. Finally he said, "I just talked to your grandma."

I nodded. My mouth was dry. I felt disoriented, detached from my brain.

"What about Aidan? Did you just say something about him?" It made my throat ache to say his name.

"Rowan, all those years ago," he started, "when you thought you were responsible for your brother's death, you weren't. Rowan, it wasn't your fault."

"It wasn't my fault?" I wished my brain would understand his words. "But I put the blanket on him."

"I know. But it wasn't your fault."

"Quit saying that!" I covered my ears. How dense could he be?

Jess stepped forward, putting herself in front of Mike. "Let's give her a few minutes. Take her home." Jess knew about Aidan. Knew all about it. One night last year, when we were smoking cigarettes Jess had swiped from her dad's car, she'd started questioning me about the rumors. I hadn't been able to talk about it, but I had been able to confirm that, yes, I had basically killed my little brother. She understood, without me even having to tell her, that I never wanted it mentioned again. Period.

"She needs to hear this now." Mike's tone was more aggressive than I could imagine coming from him.

"Cool it, guys." Dan shifted on his feet, his eyes darting between the three of us.

I was shaking head-to-toe so hard that my teeth chattered. Jess sighed and stepped back, putting an arm on my shoulder.

"I don't want to know. I'm done with that family. My mom. Dad. Trina. I'm done. There's nothing left I want to hear. There's nothing left for them to say. Dad can rot in jail. Trina can go get knocked-up by some other kid. Mom can die a slow, fat-induced death in her bed. I don't care!" I clutched my ears between my hands trying to block out the world.

Mike, with hands on my arms, leaned down until he was looking directly in my face. "Your mom killed Aidan. Not you, Rowan. It was your mom. Your Grandma told me."

"What?" I demanded.

Jess answered. "You didn't kill your baby brother, Rowan. Your mother did."

"What the hell are you talking about?" Dan demanded. "I'm going to call the police."

We ignored him.

Mike stared at me. "Your grandma told us to find you and let you know. It wasn't you. It was your mom."

"Mike, you're not making any sense." It was Dan who spoke again. "Are you saying that Rowan's mom killed that baby?"

I didn't talk about Aidan; about his death. But everyone in our small town knew about it. And knew that I was the cause. Right now, I wished more than anything in this world that Mike would stop talking about it too.

Someone's phone rang. Jess, Mike and Dan all checked their pockets. I didn't bother. The last time someone called me it was Gran telling me Trina had tried to kill herself. I didn't think I'd ever answer a phone again.

It was Jess' phone. "Hello?" she asked, brows creased. She was quiet for several moments. Then the phone fell from her ear. "Ro, your grandma is here. She wants to talk to you."

DAN MET Gran at the door, helping her inside so she didn't slip on the wet tile. Her hair was drenched from the rain. She had no coat, no umbrella. She'd been crying. Hard. Her eyes were red, her cheeks and lips pale, almost blue. She looked like someone in shock.

"Rowan…" She stopped at the door. "Did you tell her?" Her voice was strained, choked as she looked at Mike and Jess.

He nodded, his face tight. "We told her. She knows the truth now, but she needs to hear it from you."

Gran blinked several times.

No one spoke for several minutes. The whirl of the fan was the only sound. I didn't drop my eyes from Gran's, but I also wasn't sure if I was seeing her either. Mike had said something about Aidan. About my mom. And I didn't want to hear anymore. But I couldn't turn away.

"It was your mom," she whispered finally, so softly I'm not sure I heard her. "Rowan, I'm so sorry." She clutched her heart and started to sob.

"*What* was my mom, Gran?" I demanded. Mike moved to my side, putting an arm around me. "What are you talking about?" My heart pounded like a bass drum. My hands broke out in a sweat and I clenched my shirt to stop the trembling.

"Your mom, honey. She was responsible for Aidan's death. Not you."

"I…I don't understand what you're saying." My brain wouldn't work; wouldn't open and allow her words to seep in.

Gran wiped her tears and they didn't replenish, but they didn't need to. Her distress was written all over her face. In the deep lines of her wrinkles. In the creases at her eyes. In the hardness of her lips. Her shoulders shook with each breath she inhaled.

I resisted the urge to reach out to her. This was my Gran. My beloved Gran. She was hurting. Bad. And I never wanted to see my Gran hurt. But something stopped me. A need, far greater than any other I'd ever experienced, bubbled deep inside me. I needed to hear these words. I didn't want to hear these words. These words would kill me. Or kill Gran. Or create a crater underneath our feet and swallow us all alive.

"Can we talk? Alone?" She wrung her hands on her shirt.

"No." It was Jess who spoke. "Not alone."

Gran's shoulders slumped and she looked down. Just then, she looked like a ninety-year-old woman, far older than sixty-seven.

"Your mother smothered Aidan that night. She killed your brother, Rowan. Not you."

"What are you saying?" I demanded, my brain opening just a little.

"She told me the next day. After they took Aidan's body away." She held her hands out toward me, palms facing upward. "She snapped. Something in her snapped."

Dan spoke next. "Do you mean to tell me that her mother was responsible for his death? That her mother, Rowan's mother, *killed* the baby? On purpose?"

My legs gave way and Mike caught me before I fell.

Gran's lip quivered. She looked around, her eyes pleading for help. She wouldn't get any here, though.

"Gran?" Hysteria bubbled through my blood.

Her shoulders lifted and fell. "I'm sorry. Rowan, I'm so sorry. I thought I could save you both." She pulled in a quivering breath. "I thought you would be okay. That she would be okay if we handled it this way."

"It's true?" I fought to stay upright as the floor moved in waves under my feet. "Aidan dying wasn't my fault?"

She shook her head, quickly, as if she didn't want me to see it. "Aidan dying wasn't your fault," she whispered.

"But…but…why? Why did I think it was all these years? Gran?" My voice echoed off the walls in ear-piercing octaves.

"Rowan."

Words did not form inside my brain. Instead, filling up the insides was a flaming pit of red. Of rage.

I stared at her for a long, devastating time. She cowered under my stare, shrinking into herself; shrinking away from me.

"My mom killed Aidan and let me take the blame?" Each word was like a little bomb going off.

She pulled in a shuddering breath and finally nodded her head that *yes*, Mom had killed my baby brother and *yes*, she'd let me take the blame.

chapter eighteen

I BOLTED through the door and was in my car before anyone could stop me. Just as I put my foot on the gas, Mike jumped into the passenger seat. He hadn't even closed the door before I peeled out of the parking lot.

The tires screeched across the wet pavement. My fingers were white against the steering wheel. The gas pedal was all the way to the floor and the wheel shook under my grasp. Rain pelted the wind shield, the wiper blades slapping furiously.

"Rowan, let me drive."

I didn't answer.

"Rowan, slow down. You're going too fast."

I didn't ease up on the pressure.

"Rowan!" His voice was like a whip.

I glanced from the road to his face and eased my foot off the gas, letting the car slow down to just above the speed limit.

"Where are we going?" He leaned forward in the seat.

I knew where *I* was going; he just happened to be along for the ride. The silence in the car comforted me, helped me focus on the road so I didn't bother to answer him. Words did nothing but upset the natural balance of things. Words brought nothing but heartache and pain.

The tires skidded as I yanked the wheel and turned toward the hospital. My mom was standing outside the entrance to the emergency room, just under the overhang. She held a soda bottle in one hand and a candy bar in another.

I slammed on the brakes and shoved the car into park, leaving it in the middle of the road.

"Rowan, stop!" Mike's fingers brushed against my arm as I darted out of the car. But he was too late. He didn't get a grip.

Mom turned when she heard Mike yelling. Her overweight body was huddled inside one of her worn sweaters. She looked sloppy, fat, ugly.

"Is it true?" My screaming voice pierced the quiet. "Are you the one who killed Aidan? You killed Aidan?"

I was on her now, and her eyes were wide, afraid. As they should be. My own felt crazed as fury tore through me. I shoved her and she stumbled backwards. She caught herself on the bench.

"Did you kill Aidan?" I lurched over her.

"Hey, wait a minute," someone said.

"Go get the police," someone else said.

"Rowan!" Mike ran up. He grabbed my arms but I wrenched myself free.

"Is it true?" My face was inches from hers. Emotion tore through me with the force of a hurricane.

This can't be true.

This can't be true.

This can't be true.

I grabbed her sweater in my fists and shook. "Aidan's death is not my fault?"

She was crying, tears and snot running down her red, swollen face.

"Rowan!" Mike yelled. "Stop!"

A crowd gathered around.

"It's not my fault?" I screamed into her face. "Is it true?" I shook her again. "Is it true?"

She would've collapsed, fallen onto the concrete, but I held onto her sweater, shaking her back and forth like an enormous doll. I couldn't let go. My hands were gripped so tight onto her sweater that even the officer who grabbed me from behind couldn't get my hands loose.

"I hate you!"

Blubbering sobs poured from her lips and in an instant, I released her sweater and clenched my fingers around her throat.

"Let go of her!" a deep male voice shouted in my ear. "Let go of her now!"

"She killed my brother!" I squeezed her throat.

Arms that were like iron clamps yanked at me until Mom was ripped out of my hands. These same arms snapped me off my feet. I hung in the air, feet kicking at the air and hands clawing at my mom.

"Stop!" the officer boomed.

Another officer was by my mom's side. Mike stood in the space between us, his hands out and his eyes wide.

"What's going on here?" Another officer demanded.

A police cruiser pulled up, flashing lights bouncing off the side of the building.

Two more officers got out and ran toward us.

I stopped struggling and my rage settled into my eyes, shooting daggers full of poison at my mom.

"Look at me!" When she wouldn't, I shouted, "You did this!"

But she wouldn't lift her eyes to mine. I crumbled in the officer's arms. My hands dangled to my sides. My shoulders hunched. And I cried so hard I wasn't aware of anything else as the magnitude of what my mother had done, and my Gran had covered, washed over me.

I SAT on the bench, my head in my hands. At some point, one minute ago, one hour ago, I didn't know which, Mom left with two of the officers. My hearing wasn't working, though. There was nothing passing by my eardrums but a vibrating void, a noiseless noise that was so loud, I couldn't hear anything else.

But my eyes were working fine and I watched as Gran crossed the parking lot and walked toward me. She wore a raincoat now, but the hood didn't protect her from the rain as it washed over her face. Or maybe it was tears. Or maybe I didn't really give a damn.

Jess walked behind her, her cherry hair soaked and matted to her face. Gran stumbled on the sidewalk. Jess caught her before she fell. Gran looked so old, so very old. She stopped in front of me.

I glared at her, and shoved my hands in my hoodie pockets. Between my thumb and my forefinger was the thin, silver razor blade.

Her lips were moving and her hands were held out toward me. But all I could hear was a cartoon kind of sound. Something like, *wa wawawa wa.* I pulled my hood over my head and turned away.

Finally she moved over to speak to the officer standing nearby. I didn't hear a single word of their conversation and I didn't try to. Mike sat by my side, his arm around my shoulders. But I didn't feel it. I just knew, like I knew the sun was up there somewhere.

I finally dug my nails into my palms to see if I could feel it; but I felt nothing, regardless of how hard I pressed. When I bit my lip, I tasted blood but felt no pain.

"I'll be back." I jumped up.

"Where–?" Gran started to ask but stopped at the look on my face.

"Miss," started an officer, "where are you going?"

"To the bathroom," I spat.

I slipped through the automatic glass doors, an officer close behind, and into the overly bright waiting room. I darted into the bathroom.

It was quiet inside of the stall. The metal wall was cold against the heat of my palm and I rested it there for a long time–taking in, then releasing, deep breaths. My mind cleared. The anticipation built with each breath I took; the anticipation of the oncoming release. By the time I slipped my hand into my pocket and pulled out the cold, sharp razor blade, I was almost giddy.

At first I didn't feel anything. Just release. Just simple, pleasant release. I sighed. Tiny dots of blood bubbled along the line. The pain set in. The pain felt good. There was nothing else. Nothing but the pain and the release of that pain.

I exhaled, emptying my lungs until they hurt. Then I made another clean cut, connected to the other one at the end, to form a 'V.' This one was a little deeper and the shot of pain made my breath catch. My eyes teared. Finally, and with a quick slice, I connected the lines into a crooked, 'A,' unmistakable in the midst of other cuts.

I pulled out several squares of toilet paper and wiped off the razor. I threw it into the waste basket hanging on the wall. Then I pulled more paper and held it against my arm, applying pressure until the blood stopped.

"WE HAVE a few questions to ask you." Officer Randall sat across from me in the living room. It was nearly eleven at night and I was at home. Levi sat at my feet. Scout was curled in my lap. Mike sat to my right. Jess to my left.

Gran was in the kitchen, acting like she was making sandwiches. Mom was still down at the police station and I didn't know if or when she would be back. And I didn't care.

"Okay." I pulled my sleeves from my wrists down over my hands and rubbed Scout's head. Since my time in the bathroom at the hospital, I felt calmer, with a greater hold on my thoughts and my emotions. Basically, I felt numb, and that's exactly what I needed to feel to make it through this discussion.

"What do you remember of the night your brother died?"

My mouth opened, prepared to relive that harrowing time. The words swirled around, and instead of becoming a jumbled mass of pain, they settled into sentences, memories, words.

"Mom and Dad had a fight. Dad left, saying he was coming back the next day to get Aidan. He was going to leave Mom and me and Trina."

He glanced up at me from his notepad.

"Mom went to bed and locked the door. I didn't see her again that night."

"How old were you?"

"Ten."

"Your sister," he looked down at his notes, "Trina?"

"Eight."

"Was anyone else here to watch you?"

"No."

"And where was the baby? Aidan?" He glanced at his notes again.

"In his crib, asleep. Dad said he'd come back the next morning and he wanted Aidan ready."

"Did he say anything to you girls as he left?"

"No. He didn't talk much to us in general and didn't say anything that night." My words flowed on autopilot, completely buried in the past. If someone would have asked me what color the officer's uniform was, I wouldn't have been able to say. I didn't see him. I saw the house as it was seven years ago. I saw that and nothing else.

He flipped to a clean page in his notebook.

"Then what happened?"

"Mom stayed in bed all night. At one point Aidan woke up. It was time for his bottle. I made him a bottle, changed his diaper and rocked him back to sleep." A twinge of pride flickered in my heart. I had cared for him the right way. I hadn't done anything wrong. Maybe I had even done a good job.

"I put him back in his bed. Trina and I went to bed soon after that."

"Did Aidan wake up again?"

The black mass of pain wound its way into the appropriate box, where it would have to stay if I were to finish this conversation. And I realized I very much needed to finish it; to tell my story.

"No." I swallowed and rubbed the 'A,' safely hidden under the sleeve of my shirt. It was sore and I was careful not to reopen the cuts, not wanting to bleed through my clothes. "He didn't wake back up. By the morning, he was…dead."

Gran hovered nearby, wringing her hands. I didn't look at her. I didn't need to. Mike had his arm around my shoulders. I huddled in his warmth, his security. Jess was rubbing my leg. I glanced down at the nail polish that always looked so perfectly chipped, I wondered if she'd done it on purpose.

"Did you put a blanket on him?"

I patted the 'A.' "Yes. I didn't cover his face, though. I put the blanket over his lower body." I wanted to say the details. That I was careful; careful to not cover his face. I had studied that blanket for several minutes, judging that if he turned, would the blanket ride up or fall down. I had determined it would fall down toward his feet. And for all of these years, I thought I was wrong, devastatingly wrong.

"How heavy was the blanket? Is it still here?"

I shuddered. That blanket. That damned blanket. I hadn't seen it since that morning. "It was…it was…" I tried to mentally take measure of the blanket. It wasn't a baby's blanket; being a little larger than that. But it wasn't the size of a twin bed's blanket either. And it was thin. Thin, but bigger than the crib. I had bunched it up at the bottom to make sure it didn't cover his face.

"It was bigger than a baby's blanket," I finally pushed out. "But smaller than a full size."

"And what happened the next morning?"

"He was dead."

Levi curled his head back to look at me. His large chocolate eyes were wide and searching. I scratched his chin. Scout nipped at my fingers.

Officer Randall looked down at his notes, reading words someone else had already told him. Were they Mom's? Gran's? Had they interviewed Dad? Had they even found him?

What would he think about this? Did he know his wife was capable of murder? And that she was capable of laying the blame on her daughter?

After several moments of silence, he asked, "And what were you told happened?"

My shrug was painful. Scout licked my finger and I tried to smile. I really did. But I couldn't. There was not enough inside of me to push my lips upward. "I was told he died of SIDS. That it was the blanket. That he'd gotten *overheated*."

"And who told you this?" The other officer, Officer Schmidt her name tag read, finally spoke.

"My mom."

She nodded and Officer Randall looked down at his notes.

"Was there any discussion of other possibilities? That some foul play could've been involved?"

I shook my head. "No. There wasn't. Not with me. When they found out he had a blanket on…he was only two months old…and the autopsy didn't…I don't know. Nothing else was ever said. That I know of."

"And you believed all this time that you were the one responsible?"

Mike's arm tightened around me. Levi sat up straight and stared at the officer. Gran had eased into the room and stood at the armrest of the sofa. Jess turned to look at me, my hand now in hers.

"Yes. I was led to believe that I was the one responsible for Aidan's death." I stared at Gran as I said these words. The expression on her face was unreadable.

I scratched my nail over the top of my shirt, catching the wound against the fabric. I felt the skin and its fragile new scab tear. I placed my palm over my shirt and sat there in silence until the officers left and Gran went down the hall.

The officers gave Jess a ride home. I could tell she didn't want to leave. That her heart was broken. That she felt my pain. It was written in her heavily-lined blue eyes, the tears that dwelled there, illuminating them. It was written in the soft touch of her hand.

But she had to go home. And I was okay with that. I didn't want there to be any problems with her dad for her being out late.

Mike stayed by my side. If he called his home, I didn't know. But he seemed content to sit by my side and hold me long into the night.

Just me, my animals, and Mike.

chapter nineteen

IT WAS two in the morning. I stared at my ceiling, unblinking. The room was dark, except for the light of my alarm clock.

I was alone, except for my animals. Mike left around one. He offered to stay, saying he'd already let his folks know that he would be out late. I didn't ask if he told them why. But I was ready to go to bed, to be in my own space, alone with just Scout and Levi, whom I kept in the house with me.

When I heard Gran shuffling down the hall, I closed my eyes.

"Ro?" Gran peered into my room.

I hesitated, not sure if I wanted to talk to her right now. Finally, I said, "What?" and shielded my eyes from the hall's light.

She sat on my bed and reached for my leg, but I pulled away from her.

"You okay?"

"Yeah. I'm fine." There was an edge to my voice that I couldn't temper. Fury didn't begin to describe my feelings toward my Gran. She'd let me believe I had killed Aidan all these years. She'd known how the bitter resentment of Dad and Trina hovered around me everywhere I went; how I wore the guilt of killing my little brother like it was a second skin.

And still she'd let that happen.

Why?

And why didn't I tell the cops that she knew all along? Why did I feel like I had to protect her?

Maybe because she was the only family I had left.

"Do you want to talk?" she asked.

"Do *you?* There seems to be something on your mind." My tone was dry.

"Oh, Ro." She sighed as she stared out the window. The blind was up, exposing the darkness outside. "I just don't know how it came to this. Your mom has always," she paused, "struggled."

Silence settled in around me like a shroud. I needed answers, but my voice was lost to unasked questions.

She glanced at me. "Aren't you hot under all those blankets? With that hoodie on?"

I didn't respond.

She pulled in a deep breath. "Your mother attached herself to friends too easily. Even if it was clear that someone wasn't as interested in friendship as she was. Or the friendship would be going along fine, but then your mom would get close and needy. It started when she was eight. The same thing happened when she got interested in boys.

"When she was fifteen, she developed a crush on a boy at school. She wrote his name all over her notebook, used permanent marker to draw it over her skin. I think he called her a couple of times, but she smothered him and he pulled away."

Scout slept soundly by my pillow, but I craved her warmth and pulled her to me. Levi was asleep at the bottom of the bed, my feet tucked under his heavy warmth. Every now and then one of his gentle snores disrupted the quiet.

"She tried to hurt herself."

"She tried to kill herself? Like Trina?" I was suddenly oblivious to Scout or anything else. Or hurt herself like *me*? "What did she do?"

Gran bit her lip as she nodded. "She did. She just couldn't handle it. She took some pills, but I found her in her room and called the ambulance. They pumped her stomach." She pulled in a deep breath. "Just like they did Trina's.

"I found her a therapist and her life was getting on track. If she wasn't ever a *normal* teenager, she was doing okay. She had a couple of friends she saw now and then. And, when she was a senior, she developed a crush on your dad."

"Dad?"

"He was cute. A little rough around the edges, maybe, but handsome and it really seemed like he was going to make something of himself. Maybe even get out of this small town.

"Then…well," she sighed heavily again, as if the deep breaths were giving her the energy to continue. "He and your mom went out a couple of times, I guess; though I think it was mostly with a group. She wanted more. I don't think he did. And the next thing I know, your mom's pregnant. She's seventeen, pregnant, and comes home one day jubilant because your dad said he would marry her.

"It turns out his father was forcing him. Your father came from a long line of military men who did what their fathers told them, who *obeyed the rules*. And, truth be told, it was the right thing to do. It takes two to tango." She grunted. "Anyway, he was always resentful of being forced into the marriage. She was my daughter but I still understood how he could feel the way he did.

"He didn't love your mom. I think he tried to in the beginning. But it wasn't working out. So he was going to leave her. But lo and behold, she was pregnant again. His fate was sealed, so to speak."

As Gran talked, her voice changed, like the painful memories were altering her chemistry.

"And he never forgave her. He never forgave her for getting pregnant again."

"How could he put all the blame on her?"

"She lied. Told him she was taking the pill and she wasn't. She lied so she'd get pregnant again."

"But what about Aidan? Gran, why would she…" My voice broke off. How could I speak about what she did?

"Because if she couldn't make him happy, she didn't want anyone else to either." She went to the window, staring outside into the starless night. "I'm not sure. When she discovered she was pregnant again, she didn't tell your dad until she'd found out the baby was a boy. She must've known he wanted a boy. I knew he wanted a boy. It was like if he got a son, then everything would be worth it. That was the one thing I'll never forgive him for. The one thing." Her voice trailed off.

"What one thing?"

Her eyes were dark when she turned them to me. "Not realizing how wonderful you and Trina were. He never did appreciate how special you girls were; how special you are." When moisture glazed across her eyes, she turned away and wiped them with the back of her hand.

"No," she whispered. "That I'll never forgive him for."

GRAN STAYED quiet for several minutes after that last statement. Pain oozed off her body like an odor. It couldn't have been easy, watching and knowing what she did–watching her daughter entrap a man to marry her and knowing her son-in-law never did want her grandchildren.

After that conversation, a million questions still lingered in the air. But I could tell that Gran's energy was gone. She was depleted and exhausted. With stooped shoulders, she stared outside-suddenly old, fragile, weak.

I pushed back the covers. With an arm around her shoulder, I led Gran out of my room and down the hall to Mom's room, where I helped her into bed. I didn't forgive her for keeping this secret; for letting me suffer like I had been the one responsible for Aidan's death. I had flunked the fifth grade because of my misery. I began to cut myself, to carve my pain into my arm because of Aidan's death.

But if she let her granddaughter suffer to help her daughter could I blame her for that?

Right now, though, I wouldn't, *couldn't* focus on her roll in this. I tucked her into Mom's bed like a baby. And the jab of painful memory was not ignored as I pulled a blanket up to her chin and left the room. The irony of that simple act was not lost on me.

IT SEEMED the darkness of the night would linger forever, but eventually the sun rose and a new day appeared. My muscles were stiff when I got out of bed. The house was quiet without Trina and Mom…Dad. I could hear every creak of the house settling, every bird's song, even a fox off in the distance. It was a suffocating blanket of silence, not comforting, but isolating. Kind of like this house had always been.

I scooped up Scout and breathed in her scent and Levi staggered to his feet. We went down the hall. Gran was at the kitchen table sipping coffee and I was actually glad to see another person in the midst of the solitude that almost drowned me. For now, I would leave it at that; leave the judgments for later in the day, the anger. Right now I was just glad to not be alone.

"Mornin', sweetheart." Her voice was soft, hesitant, like she was weighing how to talk to me.

I glanced at her but didn't speak.

"How'd you sleep?" she asked.

I shrugged and sat Scout down. "You?"

She was silent and I glanced over. With a smirk, she shrugged her shoulders just like I had done. She tried to smile, but I turned away to fuss over Levi's collar and didn't give her a reaction. Dust from his fur filled my nose and I sneezed.

"God bless you," Gran said. "And in answer to your unasked questions, she was arrested last night. She has a hearing first thing this morning and then I'm sure they'll let her out on bail, though I don't know who will pay it." She exhaled, then said softly, as if to herself, "Me, I guess."

I nodded.

"And I haven't seen your father. I saw on the caller ID that he's called a couple of times. Have you seen or talked to him?"

I shook my head *no*. Levi scratched at the front door and I let him out.

"Has he been home since that night?"

I shook my head again, watching Levi chase after a squirrel outside. I hoped the fox was gone.

"Are you going to school today?"

God, I had school today? With everything else, I had to go to school? It seemed impossible that school was still sitting there, with its uncomfortable desks, boring teachers and angry students. It seemed so remote; so far out of reach.

But I had to go to school. And be on time. I nodded.

"Good girl," Gran whispered, as if she didn't want me to hear her words.

I glanced over at her and she was watching me with big, round, glassy eyes.

I MADE it through school that day on autopilot. Jess was there, like a death shadow just waiting on me to crack.

"Jess, you don't need to follow me. I'm fine."

She huddled over me. "I know." But she didn't move.

I sighed and went about my day. Each time I exited a classroom there she stood, waiting to escort me to my locker then on to my next class. I didn't try to dissuade her again. There was no certainty that I *was* fine, that I wouldn't crack up. Having her nearby was actually very nice. I offered a weak smile at one point, though I'm not sure that's how it turned out.

Between third and fourth period, I saw Miss J. standing outside her office, arms folded over her chest and watching the two of us move down the hall. I glanced back at her after I passed and saw her smiling and nodding toward Jess. So they were all in this together, I guessed.

I had to admit, my heart felt a weak spot just knowing that two people cared about how I made it through this day. Mike wasn't at school for some reason, but I had little doubt he'd be a shadow right along with them.

At the end of the day, I stood at my locker as Jess chattered on about Paul. I could tell she was just trying to fill the silence and Paul was the next thing on her mind, other than me.

"Thanks, Jess." Who knew that people caring about you could make even the darkest of days a little less bleak? I actually felt, if not okay, a little less filled with a sense of doom and unending pain. "I appreciate it. I really do. But you can go on now. I'm sure you have to go to work or something."

"I do, but I'll walk you to your car and then I'll go. I can be a few minutes late." Jess pushed her glasses up her nose.

"Oh, I see," I said. "Miss J. talked to Mr. Sumners? Did she give him a call?" Jess' mouth fell open, like she was surprised I knew my counselor was in on this. "Like she talked to all of your teachers today? Asking them to give you a little leeway so you could shadow your crackpot of a friend?"

"Well…" Jess blinked several times.

If I couldn't quite smile, my expression was a little less severe. "It's okay. I actually appreciate it. You're the best. Now," I slammed the locker door, "I need to get to work. I, uh, made a little bit of a mess the last time I was there and I need to make it right."

She wove an arm through mine and we walked out into the bright sunshine of an April day. The smell of flowers hung in the air, ripe from recent blooming. I inhaled deeply.

"Thanks, again. I can take it from here." I gave her a quick hug.

"I know you can. Because…" Mike came around the corner. "It's Mike's turn to take over."

I glanced between them.

"You're coming with me," he said, resolute.

"Um, I have to go to work. Are you coming with me there?"

"I can. Then you're coming home with me."

"Coming home with you?" I stared at him, my mouth hanging open.

Jess leaned forward and whispered in my ear, "I'll call you later." She slipped away.

Mike reached for my hand. "It's time for you to meet my mom."

The pit in my stomach was heavy now for a whole different reason. I sighed and got into my car, not even having the energy to argue.

chapter twenty

MIKE FOLLOWED me to work, but stayed in his car when I went inside. Dan was alone, leaning against the counter reading a magazine.

He glanced up, watching me with raised brows. "Hi, Rowan. How are you?" He straightened but didn't come toward me. "I tried to call you, to check on you."

"Yeah." I waved a hand in the air. "It's been quite a couple of days."

"That it has." Dan was guarded, not his usual flirty self.

"Dan, I'm sorry."

He didn't blink for several seconds.

"I'm sorry I came over here like that. And said those things. About marriage. It was a tough spot to put you in."

He exhaled loudly. "Rowan, I just want you to be happy. Take some time off work. You need it. I can still pay you and I can ask Mrs. Ames to take on a few more hours."

I smiled. "Thank you. I could use a break. From everything."

He nodded. "Rowan?"

"Hmm?"

"Take care of yourself."

I nodded. There was more I could say to him. But I found I didn't want to. An apology was enough.

I pushed through the door without looking back and I wasn't sure if I'd ever return.

MIKE LIVED in a proper *community*, not just a house pushed back from the road like I did. Each house was similar in that they were all large, at least twice the size of my home. The lawns were all green–mowed and encased in blooming flower beds.

The homes were built of either wood or brick, showered in sunlight, and nary a broken gutter to be seen. What had Mike thought about *my* house?

After two turns, we pulled down a short driveway that ended at a closed garage door, a huge red-brick house, and an elegant lady standing in the open doorway.

Mike pulled as close to the house as he could and I parked behind him. He got out of the car, and waved to his mom, who shielded her eyes with her hand.

She was a petite woman, with brown hair a shade lighter than Mike's. She wore dark pink pants that were cropped at her ankles, a cream-colored sweater above that and sandals below.

My heart fell to my feet, clad in scuffed black boots.

Oh my God. I don't belong here. I don't belong here. I don't belong here.

Dread bubbled through me and if I wasn't so utterly exhausted, I would've peeled right out of there.

I wasn't ready to meet his mom. Wasn't it too early for this? There was nowhere to hide, and I found I really wanted to hide right now. So I bent over in my seat, like I had dropped something and was trying to find it. Mike opened the door.

"Rowan? Come on inside."

I glanced up at him, my hand still under the seat like the imaginary missing item was there. "Okay. I'll be right there."

"Rowan," he said again, almost like he was talking to a child, but not quite. "She won't bite. You'll be surprised. She's actually really cool." He held out his hand.

I fell against the seat with a sigh and glanced toward the house. She hadn't moved from the doorway, and I was suddenly deeply grateful she was keeping her distance. If she had come to me, in the car, I think I would've vomited.

But still. I was having a hard time getting out of the car. Rowan Slone was not the kind of girl that a mom to someone like Mike Anderson would want her son to bring home.

I came with a lot of baggage. And I was only seventeen. *Good Lord.* What did the future hold if the past already held so much?

"Rowan, come on."

His hand was steady, resolute. I glanced back toward the house. His mom had gone inside. The door was still open, but the entryway was empty, summoning me like a beacon.

What would happen if I passed through that door? Entered Mike's life fully and completely? Was there room for someone like me in his life?

In the end, I really had nowhere else to go. Going back to my home, heavy with memories, resentment, and anger seemed about the worst possible option right now; even if I'd end up back there eventually, I couldn't imagine going there right now.

So, I put my hand, clammy with sweat, into Mike's and let him pull me out of the car. He started forward before I had a chance to protest. My feet were heavy, making loud *thuds* each time they hit the pavement. I felt like a zombie.

Mike chuckled and squeezed my hand. "Rowan, there's no need to be nervous. It may not be cool to think your mom is awesome, but I do. And she is."

Mike's house looked like it was straight out of a storybook about all-American happy families. The curtains weren't pulled tight. The front porch was wooden and had a little bench on it. Pots overflowing with colorful pansies sat on either side. It was a small porch, like the one at my house, but could not have been more different.

With a deep breath, we stepped inside. Mike threw his keys down on a small table. "Mom!"

The front door sucked me back to it like a vortex. I wasn't ready to meet her. She wouldn't approve of me. I wouldn't be the girl she'd want Mike to bring home. With my hands shoved deep into my hoodie pockets, I took a step back.

"Oh, no you don't." He wrapped his arms around me and started walking us forward.

Light footsteps came clacking against the wooden floor and I pushed back against Mike, trying to move us both out the front door. But then there she was, coming toward us. With a smile on her face. It was genuine, if ever a smile was. Instantly, I stopped pushing against him.

"Rowan, what a pleasure. Come in, honey." She inserted her hand between me and Mike and gently eased me inside. Mike broke away and I reached for him; but she put a hand on his back too and maneuvered both of us down a hallway to the kitchen.

It was a huge room, several times larger than the one at home. The cabinets were a pristine white; the floor's tiles soft beige. The counter was a shiny black with little specks of color. It was clean. I mean, it smelled clean. It looked clean. There was no clutter anywhere, just necessary cooking items like a few matching white jars, salt and pepper shakers, a huge bowl brimming with fruit.

"Are you hungry?" she asked.

Mike moved about the room with the ease of someone very comfortable with himself, his mom, his home. I followed him because I couldn't imagine not to. I'd live in that kitchen if I could. He sat at a breakfast table nestled near a huge bay window, and I sat beside him.

Mrs. Anderson had gentle eyes and short, perfectly styled hair. When she smiled, her white teeth, the same that Mike had inherited, shone through her pink lips. There was nothing behind her eyes, or her expression, that was anything other than welcoming. I didn't pull my hands out of my pockets but I did relax my fingers.

She flitted about the kitchen pulling out more food than I could ever imagine eating. She set down chicken, rice, cheese, crackers, ice cream and a big cup of milk. All right in front of me. It smelled amazing. Especially the chicken. My mouth watered as I forced myself not to dive onto the table. I couldn't remember the last time I'd eaten and I was suddenly hungrier than I could ever remember being.

She spooned a little of everything onto the plate in front of me, piling the mixture of food high. In a bowl she scooped out the ice cream.

"Eat." The command was gentle yet firm in a way that I was helpless to resist.

She chatted with Mike about Dr. Anderson, who was away at a dental conference. Mike nibbled on a piece of chicken and both of them politely ignored me as I ate. And ate. And ate.

My stomach ached as it expanded, but still I couldn't quit. After chowing down a large chicken breast smothered in barbecue sauce, I had two servings of rice. This was more than I'd eaten in a month put together. Somewhere in my subconscious, I was mortified with my lack of control. But I was like a starving animal, intent upon nourishing myself at the risk of everything else.

Finally, I just fell back against the chair. I swiped a napkin over my mouth, hoping it would mask my embarrassment. "Thank you," I managed. "It was delicious."

She leaned across the table and patted my hand. "I'm glad you liked it, sweetie. Cooking has become my newest passion."

Mike chuckled. "You won't go hungry here."

She flashed him a look of mock irritation, and then laughed. The sound echoed through the kitchen like the chiming of a bell. "I have four kids, and Mike is the only one left here. So, I needed a hobby. I guess I'll have to get a new one when he goes to college."

"Thank goodness she's a quick learner. In the beginning…" he widened his eyes and frowned deeply. "Yikes," he mouthed and she swatted him with a dish towel.

"I've certainly managed to feed you and your friends for the past several years and I haven't heard anyone complaining."

He rubbed his stomach. "Surely not."

I watched the two of them in their effortless banter and was blindsided with jealousy, awe, and extreme longing to have that kind of relationship with my mom. Now, though, that would never even become an option.

But my eyes were heavy. The food was making me sluggish. I had passed exhausted hours ago and now I was moving into comatose.

It must've shown because Mrs. Anderson said, "Are you ready for bed, dear? I have a room ready for you."

It was only six thirty, but my eyelids were suddenly so heavy, I couldn't hold them open. There would be no argument from me tonight. I'd sleep right there in that chair if I could. When I felt myself lifted, I barely had the energy to wrap my arms around Mike's neck and hold on.

I was asleep before he laid me in the bed. I didn't wake up until noon the next day.

I EASED the door open and peaked into the hallway. The other doors, all white, were shut. Sunlight streamed in from the large window nestled at the end of the hall and it looked like it would be a beautiful spring day.

The rug was soft beneath my feet, my toes sinking into its warmth. After staring at the closed doors, wondering which one was the bathroom, I took a step down the hall away from the window. There I found a door slightly ajar. It was the bathroom. I closed the door with a *click* and turned the lock.

It was strange to be inside of Mike's home, to have slept here. His mother was so welcoming and warm that it almost made me uncomfortable. Almost. But not quite. He was right—she was pretty cool. I didn't meet his dad last night. Mrs. Anderson said something about him being away at a dental conference. What would he think about me being here? Well, it wouldn't matter because I would leave today.

Sitting on the side of the sink was a bath towel, hand towel, and washcloth, all neatly folded. There was also a toothbrush and a tube of toothpaste and a little piece of paper that said, *Rowan*, on it.

I turned on the warm water and waited for it to heat. Then I washed my face, my hands and brushed my teeth. My reflection showed a tired face with dark circles under my eyes; lips that weren't cherry red, but pale, just slightly pink. I really did need to start eating again, though my stomach was still distended from all the food last night. But I needed to eat like that regularly. My cheekbones were so prominent, I looked skeletal.

With the sleeves of my hoodie pulled over my hands, I walked back into the hall.

The house was quiet, too quiet. No radio, television, voices. Where was Mike? His mom? Oh, how I wished he'd been waiting for me outside of the room, so I'd know what I was supposed to do.

When I made it to the bottom of the stairs, I decided to grab my keys and sneak out. I crept to the kitchen, careful not to make any noise. I made it all the way to the kitchen table before I realized I wasn't alone.

Mrs. Anderson was standing by the refrigerator, the phone to her ear as she listened to someone on the other end.

"Oh, I'm sorry," I whispered, and was about to hurry away when she started waving her hand in the air, motioning for me to come forward.

But I really wanted to leave. Badly. Mike wasn't anywhere to be seen and I didn't fancy sitting around talking to his mom. She was so nice last night, it was time to thank her for her hospitality and leave.

"Okay," she said into the phone. "Thank you."

She hung up the phone. "Good morning, Rowan. Did you sleep well?"

I nodded as I stepped into the kitchen, finding a lump in my throat that I couldn't swallow away.

"I'll make you breakfast." She pulled a plate out of the cabinet. "Mike left a little while ago. He wouldn't tell me where he was going, but that he'd be back soon. He left me instructions to make sure you were well fed this morning." She smiled and I forced a small one in return.

"I'm fine, really. I'll just get my keys and then go." I shifted on my feet. "Dinner last night was so good. I really appreciate you letting me stay here. I'll go home today. I need to check in…" My voice trailed off under the scrutiny of her gaze.

"No. You won't." She put a hand on her slender hip. "You are welcome to stay here for as long as you need to. And I fully expect you to," she waved her hand in the air, "stay here. That bedroom is yours. Period."

My mouth fell open. What did she mean? Did she want me to stay here? How much had Mike told her?

Ignoring my silence, she continued. "I've already talked to Dr. Anderson." She looked at me, her lips set. "And Mike. In fact, it was his idea and I must admit it's the best idea I've heard all month." She smiled that warm cinnamon smile again and my defenses faltered, allowing the idea to slip into my brain and form into an actual possibility. But that was crazy. I had a home.

"Besides, it will be so nice to have another young person around the house. All of my other children are away at college. And I know Mike misses having another young person around the house. Then, when he goes to college in August…I need the company. You have one more year of school, right?"

I stared at the plate of eggs she put in front of me and nodded.

She put a finger under my chin and lifted my head. "Rowan, stop those negative thoughts going through your head. I can see it written all over your face. You're to stay here for as long as you'd like. Period."

I looked away before the water that filled my eyes spilled over. Then she did something that shocked me as much as anything else. She put her hands on either side of my head and held them there a moment. I could almost feel her energy moving into me. Then she kissed me on top of the head. And once she did that, I couldn't stop the tears.

She fell to her knees in front of me and had me wrapped in her arms before a protest formed on my lips. I leaned into her spicy warmth and cried.

"Shhh," she crooned, though she wasn't telling me to be quiet. She was soothing me the same way I used to soothe Aidan, and even Trina, when she was little. With gentle rocking, pats on my back, and the endless, "Shhh, shhh, shhh," I melted into her.

My tears turned into sobs that made my stomach clench and spasm. I hiccupped several times, but she didn't let go. She stroked my hair. She rocked me back and forth. She *shhh'ed*.

The minutes flowed by as the past ripped long shreds through me. My insides were opening under the weight of those sobs, exposing everything in my life that had ever hurt. I could feel myself unraveling, coming undone cell by cell. The pain, the past, was too great. It would destroy me. I slumped against Mrs. Anderson, all the strength that had gotten me through the past several years gone.

How could my mother do that? How could she murder her child? Her beautiful little angel? Where, in her brain, did it exist–the ability to hold something over his little face and sever his breath?

How could a mother let her daughter take the blame? Wasn't I worth saving? Worth a future? She'd taken it away with the guilt and accusation. My own mother had abandoned me. My own father had never wanted me. My sister hated me. And my Gran knew all of this but did nothing to stop it.

But the pain, just at the point of breaking me, became slightly more bearable; like Mrs. Anderson was absorbing it into herself.

My sobs eased a little, became a fraction less violent. Finally I pulled back and wiped my eyes with the back of my hand.

Mike stood inside the door of the kitchen watching us. He blinked several times, then shoved his hands in his pockets.

Mrs. Anderson turned, but did not release me. "Hi, son."

"Hi." He looked at me. "I just came from your house." There was a large suitcase by his feet. A blush spread across his handsome face.

Mrs. Anderson turned to me. "Rowan, I meant it when I said you could stay here as long as you need. Even if that's until the day you graduate and leave for college. And then you have a place to come back to. I just ask that you attend church services with us on Sundays. We live a Christian life here, but we can talk about that later."

Tears started fresh and I nodded. Go to church? Like a family? Did I have anywhere else to go? Did I want anywhere else to go? My mind was attacked with questions, shooting at me like darts. What did this mean for me and Mike? Were we a couple? Were we to act like brother and sister?

But for right here, right now, I didn't let those unanswered questions take root.

"I'll take this upstairs." Mrs. Anderson kissed my head again then grabbed my suitcase, her delicate flats slapping against the tiled floor.

After she passed out of sight, Mike shuffled between his feet, hands still in his pockets. "I, ah, hope it was okay I went and got your things." He stole a glance at me.

I stood. On wobbly feet, I fell forward, right into him, into his strong arms. They wrapped around me, making me feel safer, more taken care of, and more worthy than I'd ever felt in my entire life.

epilogue

"IT DOESN'T look like me." I scrutinized the reflection in the full-length mirror. I was in a dressing room, trying on Prom dresses.

"Show me." Mrs. Anderson's feet, in a pair of strappy sandals, appeared under the door. I knew she was dying to see me in these dresses, but I hadn't shown her a single one. She had patiently passed alternate styles, sizes and options over the top of the changing room door, all while getting no visual in return. I just couldn't. Not with my arms so exposed.

When I didn't answer, she asked, "Does it fit?"

I studied the girl in the mirror. The dress color was labeled as *mint green* but it wasn't what I would consider mint. It wasn't a rich, bold color, but rather, a very light green, almost a whisper woven within the fabric. It had tiny, delicate straps that went over my still thin, yet fuller shoulders. The neckline was straight across, a few inches below my collarbone. The strapless bra that Mrs. Anderson had sent me into the changing room with gave me more curves than I'd ever had in my life.

Under Mrs. Anderson's care, though, I'd gained about eight pounds, and had filled out a little. My hair was glossier, healthier. She'd taken me for a haircut last week and now I had layers that fell in soft, silky brown waves.

My skin was clearer, too, rosier. Even my posture was better, though I wasn't sure why. But for some reason, I stood straighter, which helped me look taller than I was. The image staring back at me was beautiful; more beautiful than I could have ever expected.

Except for one thing: the scars that ran along my arm. Though faded, the 'A' I'd carved into my skin was as visible as any scar could be. It was deeper than the other cuts, bolder; a blaring reminder of the path I'd traveled.

There was no way I'd wear this dress; not with the scars. And when I went to the Prom with Mike, I wanted to look beautiful. Not like a hacked-up piece of wood.

"It doesn't fit." I stared at my arm in the store's overly bright lights, seeing the scars reflected back at me in the mirror. Suddenly, they were all I *could* see.

I hadn't cut myself since that day at the hospital and I hoped I never would again. But the scars would stay engraved in my skin, a constant reminder of the girl who had thought she'd killed her brother; the girl whose mother let her take the blame; the girl who came out of an awful experience and managed to try and remake who she was.

"Should I get something else?" There was no end to her patience.

The dress was elegant in its simplicity. It fell just above my knees and with knees not quite as bony as they used to be, the dress put my more shapely legs on perfect display. It was drawn in at the waist with a satin belt, two shades lighter than the dress.

If it weren't for the scars, it would have been perfect.

I stepped closer to the mirror, inches from the smooth glass. The changes in my life that came with living with Mike and his family shone back at me from my gray eyes. Before they were dull and lifeless, now they were bright. The white was whiter; the gray richer. I had never seen it before, never noticed, but there was a blue undertone to the color, as if they really were like a stormy sea—stormy gray on the surface, deep blue underneath.

Mrs. Anderson had shown me the right way to apply mascara and it really made my eyes pop. I also had on a light swipe of blush and colorless lip gloss.

I'd been with the Andersons for a month. I hadn't returned home for any reason. Mike had not only retrieved my clothes, but he and his dad had retrieved Scout and Levi, welcoming them into their home. Mike's bulldog, Delilah, had shown a few moments of jealously but quickly got over it when she realized Scout and Levi weren't out to take over her queen bee status. Levi was even allowed to stay in the house in my room. He slept at the foot of my bed. Scout slept on the pillow by my head.

There were still many things going on with my family. Trina. Mom. Dad. I tried to keep away from them all. I wasn't ready to go back there. In any sense. Not yet.

I was in phone contact with Gran, who, when she tried to give me updates on my family, I shut down with a curt *no*. The pain was too real and my wounds too raw.

But for today that life seemed almost part of an alternate universe, a separate plane of existence. The only reminder being the scars that covered my skin; the constant reminder that life was cruel and we all did the best we could to handle what we'd been given.

I didn't need to know what happened to my mother. Mike knew. His parents knew. Of course Gran knew what was going on. But anytime someone tried to talk to me about it, I shut them down with a swipe of my hand: *Don't go there*. It was not the time to know. I knew more than enough already and it had nearly pushed me over the edge. I deserved a little bit of time simply *not knowing*.

Besides, this was never Mom's story. It wasn't Trina's. Dad's. Or even Aidan's. It was my story and it always had been.

"Rowan?"

I stepped back from the mirror and studied my reflection one more time.

"Mrs. A., do you think there is a shawl or sweater than can go over this? I think I'll get, um, cold without one. But," I nodded to my reflection, "I change my mind. I love this dress."

Without missing a beat, Mrs. Anderson threw a new garment over the door. I caught it and hung it up by the hangar. It was a sweater made of the softest, most luxurious fabric that had ever been between my fingers. It was pale ivory, almost white but not quite, and it shimmered, ever so slightly, under the overhead lights.

I pulled it on. The sleeves didn't reach my wrists, but they weren't supposed to. They came halfway between the crook of my elbow and my wrist bone; long enough to cover my scars but not so long as to be bulky over such a whimsical dress.

The front had no buttons, leaving most of my collarbone and chest visible. It fell just above the waist of the dress.

"It's perfect." My eyes filled. With a deep breath, I opened the door and let Mike's mom see me. The tears in her eyes told me more than words ever could.

"OH MY God, Rowan, you look amazing." Mike, dressed in a black tuxedo, white shirt, black bow-tie and cummerbund, stood at the bottom of the stairs. His hair, grown a little longer over the past month, was still damp from his shower. He stared at me, a pink rose corsage held in his hands.

His parents were behind him, their arms wrapped around each other. Mrs. A. leaned her head onto Mr. A.'s shoulder. They were both smiling.

Mike's older sister, Tabitha, stood behind me and I knew she was smiling too. She had become a fast, and very dear friend from the first time she'd come home from college to visit. Now we talked on the phone regularly and emailed or texted all the time. She was only a little bit bigger than me, now that I had gained some weight, and we could even share clothes, though it was mostly me borrowing hers and not the other way around.

Tabitha had helped me get ready; had come home for the weekend just for that reason. She'd conditioned, combed and dried my hair into a glossy sheen. The sides were pulled away from my face and held with a crystal clip. She'd applied more makeup than I was used to, but it was still subtle and I was okay with it. In fact, as I walked down the stairs, I felt more beautiful than I ever had in my entire life. I stopped in front of Mike and looked up at him.

He was so handsome, I almost lost my breath. He'd always been very good looking; but something about the way he was dressed tonight, about the way he looked at me, made my knees go all wobbly and my stomach do flips.

And for a moment, just a brief moment, there was no one else in the world but me and Mike.

But then Mr. A. cleared his throat and we all laughed. I actually laughed, something I'd done more of lately. Pictures took about thirty minutes and included every pose imaginable. There were a few of Tabitha and Mike, of Tabitha and me. I took pictures of the four of them together. It was all so easy and relaxed, it felt alien somehow.

I still had trouble accepting their hospitality. And I didn't know if I would stay or not. Mike would graduate in a few weeks and though he'd spend the summer here, he'd leave in late August for college on a soccer scholarship. I didn't know where that left us; didn't want to think about it.

Right here, right now, I was okay. My scars were still there, but they were healed as well as they would ever be. I hadn't held a razor between my fingers in a month. And it felt good. If I was sad, or upset, I would go for a walk, or play with Levi and Scout. Or curl onto Mike's lap and let him stroke my hair.

Mrs. A. had gotten me an after school job at the animal shelter. I threw myself into that job with an earnestness that had me getting there early, leaving late and coming in, unscheduled, on the weekends. But it felt right. Just me and the other *unwanteds* of the world.

But I didn't feel unwanted. I felt, if not a part of a family, at least a close friend of one. And that was okay.

"IT'S TIME for you two to go," Mr. A. said.

"Oh, just one more!" Mrs. A. scurried toward us. "Now, Mike, you stand here. Rowan, face him." She posed us inches apart, face-to-face. She placed Mike's hands on my waist and mine on his shoulders.

"Uh-oh," laughed Tabitha. "Here it comes."

"Here what comes?" I pulled my lip between my teeth.

"The kissing picture." Mike groaned as he put his head in his hand.

"What?" I pulled back.

"Oh no you don't." Mrs. A. laughed as she gently pushed me back into his arms. "Just a little peck." Then she swatted Mike on the shoulder. "Just a peck."

It was the chastest kiss that had ever occurred on Prom night.

Just as we walked outside, Jess and Justin, her date for the Prom, were leaving his house two doors down from Mike's. She was still dating Paul, but they had talked about Prom and decided he couldn't be the one to take her. So, Mike had set her up with Justin, and Jess was going to meet up with Paul later. I still didn't approve, but I was so glad to have her here tonight sharing this with me that I decided to keep the *Paul* comments to myself.

Justin was dressed almost identical to Mike, and almost looked as handsome. Almost. Jess had on a short dress that fell mid-thigh. The top was black satin with thick shoulder straps. The skirt was multi-layered with alternating sheets of deep purple and black. Her cherry red hair had rainbow streaks in it and for tonight, she wore her contact lenses. She looked amazing.

"My God, Ro, you look incredible!"

"Oh, Jess, you look beautiful!" We hugged while the guys laughed and shifted on their feet, growing warm in their heavy suits.

"Come on, ladies. It's a sauna out here." Justin wove Jess' arm through his, pulling her from me. We didn't release our hold on each other, though, catching hands while the guys escorted us toward the black limousine Mr. A. had rented for the night.

We piled in and I felt almost giddy, like Cinderella going to the Ball. When it turned midnight, would this all become a dream? An unreality that I had conjured in my desperation?

Then Mike was kissing me. Long and sweet, with promises of more to come. Much more to come, though when I didn't know.

As the car pulled away, I broke the kiss and looked out the window. It was a cloudless evening, the sky colored powder blue. My heart lurched at the sheer perfection; only this time, I didn't clutch my arm and my heart didn't wither under the pain. Instead, I said a prayer for my sweet baby brother. I pulled his image into my mind, not the one of him in death, but the one of him in life: gurgling, cooing, wrapping his chubby fingers around mine, smiling his first smile.

Then I looked back at Mike and found his eyes on me. With a whisper of a touch, he brushed his fingers over the top of my hand, sending shivers up my arm. He smiled. I nodded and didn't have to force the upswing of my lips.

We sped down the road with the past trailing us, if not far behind, then at a distance and nothing but open road ahead.

acknowledgments

There are many people who have supported me through the writing and publication of this book. I'd like to thank: Kathy, Randi, Melissa, and Chris for reading it and giving me valuable feedback; Juliette, Marion, and Tara for being wonderful writing friends; my friends and family who have been there for me through this process. A simple question, a kind statement, a word of encouragement have meant so much. I appreciate it more than you know.

I'd like to give a shout-out to the Yanas—you know who you are. You gals rock!

Many thanks to my husband who believed in this book from the beginning and championed it each step of the way. I love you, baby.

To my grandma, who is one of the strongest, most beautiful women I know.

And finally, I'd like to thank my amazing mom. She is my inspiration, my support, and my very best friend. Thanks, Mama, for all that you do and for being you.

about the author

Tracy Hewitt Meyer is an award-winning author of young adult fiction. Much of her work centers around the challenges teenagers face, and she has tackled the topics of pregnancy, self-harm, and transgender. She holds a B.A. in English and a Master of Social Work. Her other work includes *The Reformation of Marli Meade*, which earned a Gold Medal for Best Regional Fiction from the Independent Publisher Book Awards. Her short story on transgender, "Tender is the Deception," appears in the YA anthology *On the Edge of Tomorrow*. Tracy lives in Virginia with her husband and two children.

CPSIA information can be obtained
at www.ICGtesting.com
Printed in the USA
FSHW021540260220
67566FS